BRATVA KING'S BRIDE

KRYSTAL CLARK

Copyright © 2025 by Krystal Clark

All rights reserved.

No part of this book may be reproduced in any form or by any electronic or mechanical means, including information storage and retrieval systems, without written permission from the author, except for the use of brief quotations in a book review.

INTRODUCTION

All characters in this book are over 18 years of age. This book contains explicit scenes and situations, including kinks and themes that will be triggering to some people such as: breeding kink, a big age gap between the main characters, pregnancy, noncon, rough sex, dominant MMC, and one instance of mild breathplay. If you have issues with any of these, don't read.

ONE

Zorina

THE FIRST NOTE spills from my violin like silk. Sweet, aching, and trembling with longing. The theater hushes under my fingers, a thousand strangers holding their collective breath as I pour everything—every fractured dream, every hollow ache, every stolen hope—into the melody.

I am alive here, on this stage. Under the golden lights, wrapped in the hum of music that shields me from the world beyond these velvet walls.

But I feel him.

Even before I see him, my body knows. A ripple under my skin, a flicker of awareness coiling tight in my stomach. My gaze sweeps across the sea of faces, past the shimmering evening gowns and tailored suits, and stops—there, front row center.

Misha Antonov.

My fiancé. My storm.

Even in the half-light, he commands attention. He doesn't

smile, doesn't applaud between sets like the rest of them. He just... watches. Dark eyes pinned to me, jaw tight, massive frame sprawled in that seat like the ruler he is. There's something terrifying and beautiful about him—polished brutality wrapped in the finest suit money can buy.

The strong cut of his jaw, sharp enough to carve through steel, sits tight and unyielding. Brown hair, thick and slightly tousled, like he'd run frustrated fingers through it before arriving. And those eyes—stormy, impenetrable gray—lock on mine with the force of a tidal wave, pulling me under, holding me captive.

He draws me in effortlessly but I know he doesn't intend to. He's just intense by nature. That passion in his eyes, those torrents of depth...they're not for me. I'm just the wife he has to marry to secure an alliance.

The bow falters in my hand for half a heartbeat before I correct it, my muscles tightening to keep the music steady. The music flows, but inside, I'm already undone.

He's come to see me perform before, though rarely. I never know when. Never expect him. But when he's here, every note feels like it's carved directly from my soul for him.

I tell myself it's gratitude. Misha signed me to his label when I was a nobody. Paid for my college. Assigned his most trusted men to shadow me wherever I go, keeping me safe from the world my father controls. He gave me everything. My career, my independence.

A tremor slips through my wrist and I correct it swiftly, channeling the weakness into the music's rising crescendo. This concert—this full house, this spotlight, this triumph—it all exists because of him.

I remember the first time he stood up for me, the first time he stepped into the war zone that was my family and dragged me out, cradling my dreams in his iron fist.

I was eighteen, back then. Just a girl who wanted to play music, who didn't want to be auctioned off to some old Bratva ally for power. But I had already been promised to him and our engagement ring glinted on my finger, a five-carat diamond as shiny as it was heavy.

"Violin is a distraction," my father had sneered across the cold marble expanse of our dining room. His rings had glinted on his thick fingers, his eyes—so much like my brothers'—had burned with contempt. "No daughter of mine will waste herself parading on a stage. You will marry where I tell you. You will carry children. That is your place."

I'd choked back tears, my knuckles white around the slim neck of my violin, my voice trembling. "It's just one audition, Papa. One opportunity—"

"Enough." His hand had come down like a thunderclap against the table. "I will not hear this foolishness again."

I remember running, heart splintered, dreams bleeding out. I remember the despair, the helpless fury of knowing my life wasn't mine to live.

Back then, I was young. Bold. Rebellious. I didn't want a no. I wanted freedom. Independence. I wanted to shine on stage, to be seen to be heard, to be more than a wife trapped in a golden cage.

So I went to the last man I should have trusted. My last resort. My fiancé.

Desperation twisted in my chest. I was ready for the worst.

I remember standing at the door of Misha's penthouse, trembling with nerves, clinging to my violin case like a lifeline. I'd told myself I was crazy. He was Bratva royalty, my future husband... and barely knew me.

But I'd rung the bell anyway.

The door had swung open after a moment, and I'd nearly forgotten how to breathe.

Misha stood there, barefoot, half-naked, fresh from a shower. A towel sat low on his hips, water droplets clinging to golden skin stretched over sculpted abs and a chest built like something out of my forbidden daydreams. Brown hair damp and unruly, stubble shadowing his jawline.

God help me, I'd never seen anything more sinful. My pussy throbbed so hard, I felt moisture running down my thighs. My reaction shocked me. It was so visceral, so potent. With just a glimpse of his strong, dominant body, he could set my body on fire.

His gray eyes narrowed. "Zorina?" His voice was pure steel, rough from disuse. "What the fuck are you doing here?"

I swallowed hard, cheeks flaming. "I... I need your help."

His gaze flickered to the clock behind me, lips pressing into a thin line. "At midnight?" He looked around and frowned. "You came alone. That's dangerous and reckless."

"I had no other choice." I gathered my fraying thoughts into a coherent sentence. My heart was hammering in my chest. Proximity to Mikhail, "Misha" made my knees shake with both fear and arousal. "I ran away from home to meet you."

He cleared his throat, faint amusement twinkling in his eyes. His mouth curved up slightly as he placed his hand—warm and reassuring—on my shoulder. "Well, I didn't expect that. And why, exactly, did you want to see me in the middle of the night?"

"I..." My throat closed. "I have a favor to ask of you. I didn't know who else to go to. My father—he said I have to stop playing the violin... he said I belong in your bed, not on a stage. But I've spent my entire childhood practicing the violin, dreaming of a career in music. We're not going to be married for a few years, at least. I want to play until then. Professionally."

Misha's jaw ticked, muscle flexing as his eyes darkened. I

flinched involuntarily, afraid he'd reject me outright for being daring enough to request such a thing. Most bratva princesses who got arranged marriages were content to spend their husband's money and live a lavish life wearing designer clothes. They didn't ask for more, because more was never given to them.

But I refused to be one of them.

Then, before I could blink, he stepped aside. "Come in." His voice didn't give away any emotion but relief flooded my chest. He was at least open to the idea.

I stepped past him, inhaling a mix of cedarwood and crisp soap, heart galloping as his hand landed on my shoulder, firm and commanding.

"Sit," he ordered, steering me toward a chair. He raked his gaze over my body, lighting up my nerves. "You want to drink something?"

I shook my head. "No, I just want you to give me your word that you'll let me pursue my passion for music. My father can't say anything if you approve."

Mikhail closed his eyes. He looked vulnerable for a second, and he was the kind of man who always looked like he could snap a person's neck at the slightest provocation. It surprised me to see him like this—hair wet from a shower, a towel around his waist, looking so normal inside his home.

"Play for me," he said finally.

Nerves tangled in my chest. "What?"

His eyes cut to mine, cold and impatient. "You said you wanted to play professionally. Convince me you're not wasting my time."

I sat, knees trembling, fingers fumbling with the violin's neck. He stood in front of me, arms crossed over his bare chest, imposing and expressionless.

If I messed up, I'd humiliate myself in front of the man I

was promised to marry. I expected him to be cold. Cruel, even. My father always was.

But Misha never threatened me. Never raised his voice.

Still... he terrified me.

I drew the bow across the strings, the first few notes shaky before muscle memory took over. Slowly, the melody filled the room, soft and aching, every note bleeding my desperation, my dreams, my hope.

When the final note fell silent, I finally looked up, heart in my throat.

Misha's arms dropped to his sides, the faintest flicker of something—approval?—crossing his otherwise unreadable face.

"Okay," he said simply, walking to his phone. "I'll sign you to Stars Entertainment."

I blinked. "What?"

"You heard me." He glanced over his shoulder, grabbing his phone. "Tomorrow morning, you'll meet the label's CEO. You'll play for him, and then you'll join a conservatory so you can improve your skills and acquire prestigious credentials."

"Why?" The word spilled out, breathless and confused. "Why would you do this?"

Misha turned back, gray eyes sharper than blades. "Because you wear my ring. Because you'll be my wife. And when you come to me, Zorina..." His lips curled, almost... threatening. "I want you to come without regrets."

My pulse thudded in my ears.

"And..." His tone dipped, almost too low to catch. "You have talent. I want to see what you can do."

My lips parted, a thank you choking in my throat. I'd spent my life under my father's thumb, crushed beneath his expectations, never good enough for his approval.

And in one night... Misha shattered that cage.

A girl could fall in love with a man like that. And maybe I

did. Maybe I did fall for my future husband because I haven't been able to stop dreaming of him touching me ever since. I haven't stopped wondering if he'll be as gentle in bed as he was to me that day.

"Thank you," I whispered, the words feeling too small, too inadequate.

He shrugged, as if signing me to one of the most prestigious entertainment companies in the country was just another Tuesday. He owned several record labels, hotels, and casinos. He controlled his family's 'legal' empire that consisted of movie production, music, and leisure venues like hotels, resorts, and casinos. He was incredibly rich, probably a multi-millionaire, and yet, he was also young, barely thirty. So much responsibility on his shoulders. "You'll sleep here tonight. It's too late to drive back. I'll call your father."

I froze, panic flaring. "You—here? With you?"

Misha raised a brow, looking every inch the jaded, untouchable man he was. "Relax, malyshka. I'm not going to touch you. You'll be a virgin on our wedding night."

Still, when I brushed past his bare arm, my skin sizzled.

He pulled away instantly, shaking his head like he was annoyed with himself. "Get some sleep. You'll need it."

I swallowed. "I won't forget this. Thank you."

Misha's gaze softened, the smallest crack in his ice. "I'll sleep well tonight... thanks to your music."

And just like that, he turned and left me alone, leaving me with a beating heart, trembling fingers, and the first taste of what it felt like to be truly... seen.

After that, I went to a prestigious conservatory in Moscow. I practiced till my fingers bled. When I graduated, I released a classical crossover album with his record label. It was hugely successful, making me a rising star in the world of classical music. Since then, I've been playing sold-out tours across North

America and Europe. But of late, I've confined myself to Las Vegas, taking up a residency at one of the casinos Misha owns.

I'm twenty-four now. I promised I'd marry him at twenty-five. That means I have to start preparing for my wedding. Start preparing to be his wife.

And yet... it's more than that.

There's a hunger I can't kill. A foolish, hopeless little yearning that thrums in my blood whenever I catch my fiancé looking at me like this. Like I'm his... but never close enough to touch.

My fingers fly across the strings, drawing out the last haunting note, letting it hover in the still air before silence drops. The applause roars, thunderous and bright, but my eyes stay on him. Waiting. Wishing.

He doesn't clap. His lips don't so much as twitch. But his gaze... it burns.

A strange, needy heat rushes through me, making my knees wobble as I stand to bow.

For a moment, I forget the world outside this theater exists. I forget my father's rigid commands. My brothers' cold indifference. I forget the way I'm passed between powerful men like some fragile porcelain token of allegiance.

For one fleeting second, I imagine I'm just a woman. A woman who belongs to him.

Then thunderous applause drags me back to the grim reality.

It's a standing ovation, the crowd in the Grand Casino Theatre losing their minds over my performance, but Misha sits there like stone, broad shoulders relaxed, long legs stretched out in front of him. A king watching his property perform.

A little part of me aches anyway, even though I should be used to this by now.

My heart is such a traitor.

I step off stage, my palms still damp around the violin case, muscles burning with the effort of standing poised for an hour straight. The casino's private staff guide me through the back corridor toward my dressing room. Fans scream in the distance. Journalists wait at the barricades.

But I only wonder if Misha is still sitting there, still watching me.

The door shuts behind me with a soft click, muffling the outside world. I suck in a shaky breath, finally letting my shoulders sag, pressing my fingers to the spot above my racing heart.

It's done.

My first concert after the album release. Every seat sold out. Every critic eating out of my hand. Everything Misha built for me.

And yet...

"Zorina," a familiar, velvety voice croons from the corner of the room.

I freeze.

Victor is leaning against the dressing table, arms crossed, watching me like a man starving. His dark blond hair is tousled, his sharp jaw dusted with five o'clock shadow, the smile on his face equal parts lazy and hungry.

"You were flawless," he says, stepping closer, voice dropping to something huskier. "No... you were breathtaking."

I exhale slowly, setting my violin down before turning to face him, keeping my distance. "Thank you," I say politely, forcing a smile. "That means a lot."

Victor's been with me since the beginning, assigned as my manager the moment I signed to Misha's label. He's good at his job. Loyal. Helpful. And I know exactly what he wants when he lets his gaze trail down my body.

"You don't have to be alone tonight," he murmurs, moving close enough for me to catch the faintest whiff of expensive aftershave. "We could... celebrate. I could help you unwind."

It's tempting.

Pathetic, but tempting.

I've spent six years pining after a man who never so much as touches me, while another offers everything I claim to crave—attention, affection, desire.

I open my mouth, unsure of what's about to come out.

"Get out."

The growled command cuts through the room like a blade, making me jolt.

Victor straightens, his entire face draining of color as Misha steps into the room like a storm front, tall and furious, tailored suit immaculate, jaw sharp enough to break skin.

"Out," Misha repeats, voice lethal, eyes narrowed.

Victor stammers, "I—I was just congratulating—"

"Now," Misha snaps, every inch of him radiating ice-cold fury.

Victor bolts like a kicked dog, slinking out of the room without daring to meet my eyes again. The door clicks shut behind him, and suddenly the room feels smaller. Hotter.

I swallow, backing up until my calves brush the edge of the vanity stool. "You didn't have to scare him like that."

Misha turns his head toward me, gray eyes raking down my body like he's making sure I'm still intact. "Yes, I did."

My pulse spikes, cheeks flushing under the weight of that possessive stare. I cross my arms over my chest, trying to hold myself together. "Did you enjoy the concert, Mr. Antonov?"

The corner of his lip twitches. "Not your best."

My jaw drops. "Excuse me?"

He shrugs, walking closer, his stride slow, calculated, like a predator cornering prey. "You were off tempo during the second movement. And your bow trembled during the fifth."

My mouth opens to snap back but then closes because... damn it, he's right. Of course he's right. He's always listening, always paying attention, even when he looks bored out of his mind.

"Fine," I mutter. "Next time I'll be perfect. For you."

His gaze sharpens. "Good girl."

The praise knocks the air right out of my lungs. Heat curls in my belly, radiating down to my core, filling me up with warmth and excitement. My knees wobble slightly as currents run under my skin.

I have no idea why I always act like a horny teenager when I'm with my fiancé. Other men have praised me countless times, but it never made a dent. Misha's praise means something. He doesn't dole out compliments freely. Only when I really deserve them. That makes them special.

"Tuesday," he says, changing the subject with a precision that makes my head spin. "We'll go to Van Luxor's."

My brows furrow. "The jeweler?"

He nods, casually tugging on his cufflink, muscles flexing beneath the tailored sleeve. "You're free on Tuesday. No performances, no rehearsals. I checked your schedule."

Of course he did.

"And why are we going to a jeweler?" I ask, even though a part of me already knows. His patterns are predictable—controlled generosity, meticulous planning, fulfilling duties because it's expected of him.

"For the wedding," Misha replies simply, shrugging like it's the most obvious thing in the world. "You'll need something to wear for the after-party. A necklace, maybe earrings... something that belongs to you, not your father."

Something that belongs to me.

The words tangle around my ribs and tighten.

"You've already given me everything," I whisper, shaking

my head. "You paid for my schooling, gave me my career, assigned me protection... you don't need to keep—"

"It's not about need," Misha interrupts sharply. His gaze drops to my lips, lingers there too long, making my heart jolt in my chest. "It's about what's mine."

Heat licks up my spine, pooling low in my belly, twisting me into knots I don't want to unravel.

My voice turns softer. "You don't have to keep... buying me."

"I'm not buying you, Zorina," he says, voice like steel wrapped in silk. "I already own you. There's nothing to buy."

My throat dries out completely.

I press my palms to the cool vanity behind me, needing the grounding before I do something reckless. Like press my lips to his, or slide my hands up his chest just to feel those hard lines beneath his shirt.

A harsh laugh spills from my mouth. "I guess you're right. In a few months, I'll be off stage and you'll own me completely."

"You're quitting music?" His eyebrow slides way up his forehead. He's surprised by my words, even though I imagined he'd have expected them. "Why?"

"I want to stay at home after we're married."

Gray eyes flicker to me, sharp and assessing. "Did your father decide that?"

I shake my head. "No. I did."

His jaw clenches tighter. "Why?"

Because I'm tired of performing for rooms full of strangers when the only man I care about never even claps. Because I want love, not standing ovations.

I give him a safer answer. "Because it's exhausting. The constant travel, the nerves, the spotlight... I just want to play when I feel like it. Not because I have to."

Something flickers in his gaze, something unreadable. "So what will you do after we're married? Stare at the walls all day?"

"I'll be your good little Bratva wife," I tease, even as my voice cracks under the weight of how much I want him to fight me on it. To say I'm more than that. "Stay at home, look pretty, have your babies. You know."

He growls, unimpressed by my response. Maybe it's too generic for his liking or he doesn't believe me. After all, I'm the same woman who stormed into his house at night, a few months after our engagement and demanded that he let me play professionally. We were supposed to get married when I turned twenty-one, but thanks to my college education and budding music career, our wedding was pushed back multiple times.

My father put his foot down, telling me to get married at twenty-five or he'd break the deal with the Antonovs. I didn't want to inconvenience Misha after all that he has done for me, so I agreed in a heartbeat.

Something shifts in Misha's expression—subtle but unmistakable.

Disappointment.

My chest tightens.

I was supposed to make him happy saying that, wasn't I? That's what the men in my life have always wanted. Compliance. Obedience. Silence.

But Misha doesn't smile. He just watches me like I've disappointed him in a way I don't fully understand.

"Thanks to you, I got a taste of the independence I craved." I have a lot of money saved up in my bank account. Enough to live a modest life. Not that I'll ever use it. But performing professionally for years has fulfilled my dream. I don't want to do this all my life. I want my life to be filled with more: travel, family, love, passion, children…and I think I'm ready to let this go so I can have what I really crave.

"So all this was just for a fleeting taste of independence?" he inquires, voice sharp as a dagger.

I force out a laugh, brushing invisible dust from my skirt. "You're just upset because you put too much money into my career and I'm tossing it away."

"No," Misha says quietly, but the edge in his voice cuts through me, sharp and unrelenting. "I already got my investment back. And I made a profit on it, too."

"That's great, isn't it?" I toss my head back, exhaling loudly. "Now I can retire without any regrets."

He doesn't reply. He takes a step back, exhaling harshly, running a hand through his dark brown hair before turning for the door.

And I'm left there, burning, aching, wishing he'd pull me closer instead of walking away. Wishing he'd hug me, kiss me, tell me he can't wait for our wedding. Can't wait to make love to me.

But he doesn't do any such thing.

Because that's what he always does—saves me, builds me up… then leaves me starving for more.

"Tuesday. Van Luxor's. 10 a.m. My men will pick you up from your father's house. Don't be late," Misha says, glancing over his shoulder before walking out.

And I know, deep in my bones, that every time I think I have Misha Antonov figured out… he's going to remind me I don't know a damn thing about him.

TWO

Misha

SHE DOESN'T UNDERSTAND.

I watch the door close behind me, my fingers curling into fists as I stalk down the corridor. My body's tight, coiled like a wire pulled taut. Every muscle in my chest aches from restraint.

Zorina doesn't have a clue what she does to me.

I can smell her perfume on my jacket. Hear her soft, breathy voice lingering in my ears, taunting me. Those big brown eyes looking up at me like I could crush her with a word —or lift her to heaven if I ever bothered to try.

And maybe I could.

But I won't.

I slam the SUV door shut and lean back against the seat, exhaling hard, trying to shake her off. The driver says something but I don't register it. My thoughts are full of her— standing in that dressing room, cheeks flushed from the performance, lips still red from playing the violin, chest rising and falling like she'd just survived a storm.

I told myself this was an arrangement. She was a deal. A necessary alliance.

So why the fuck did it feel like I was standing there, leashed, barely keeping myself from throwing her over my shoulder and dragging her back to my penthouse?

I grit my teeth, shifting in my seat, adjusting the tightening in my pants. God, she was flirting. The shy little smiles, the teasing about being a "good Bratva wife," the way her throat worked when I touched her wrist.

But it wasn't the flirting that wrecked me—it was the way she looked like she needed me to see her. Like she was begging for something I didn't know how to give.

I slam my fist into the armrest, jaw ticking.

Leo's words echo in my skull: *You don't marry a woman like her just to keep her in a box.*

No. I'll marry her because I swore to my brother I'd protect our family, secure the alliances, grow the empire. That's what this is. Strategy.

Except... every time I see her on stage, I feel something burn beneath my ribs. Something dangerous. Something I buried a long time ago after losing Rolan, after seeing what happens when you care too much in this world.

Care gets you killed.

Feelings make you reckless.

And I'm already reckless where Zorina is concerned.

My hand slides into my pocket, thumb grazing the worn edges of an old photograph. Rolan's smile stares back at me—carefree, arrogant. Young. Dead. All because of me.

I clench my fist around the photo, forcing the emotion back down into the black pit where it belongs.

I saved Zorina because she came to me five years ago with

wide, desperate eyes, begging to play music when her father wanted her locked up and popping out heirs. I funded her career because she deserved a life that wasn't dictated by that cold bastard's fist. I gave her everything because it was my duty to make sure she didn't end up broken like the rest of the girls I grew up seeing in this world.

But she's not supposed to haunt me.

Not supposed to tempt me every time her lips part or her hips sway or she smiles like she has no idea she owns me without even trying.

I rake a hand through my hair and let my head fall back, staring up at the roof of the car.

I'll buy her whatever she wants at Van Luxor's on Tuesday. Cover her neck in diamonds so no man ever looks there again. Mark her wrists with sapphires so no other bastard thinks he can touch her skin. Lock her in my name, in my world, in my control.

Because Zorina Morozov was promised to me.

And by the time our wedding day comes, she'll understand exactly what it means to be mine.

Even if I burn for her in silence.

Even if I can never let her know just how deep this obsession runs.

THREE

Zorina

THE MOROZOV MANSION looms before me like a testament to everything I hate and everything I can't escape. Stately, imposing, carved from polished ivory stone, with tall columns and sprawling balconies meant to showcase power. Cold, elegant... hollow.

I walk through the wrought-iron gates, past fountains that glisten under the dying sun, their marble angels spouting water into silence. The moment my heel clicks against the glossy floors, the air thickens, pressing down like a velvet noose.

"Zorina," my mother's voice floats from the grand staircase, her tone always sharp beneath its sweetness.

I glance up. Tatiana Morozov descends like a movie star in a pearl-studded silk gown, every hair pinned perfectly into place, her diamonds catching the chandelier light. Beautiful, ageless, and utterly hollow.

She reaches me, air-kissing both cheeks, and the

critique comes immediately, like clockwork. "Darling, your posture is slipping again. If you want to keep Misha interested, you should act more... refined. You're still too spirited."

Translation: Be small. Be agreeable. Be forgettable.

"Of course, Mother," I murmur, because it's easier than arguing.

We glide into the sitting room where gold accents drown the walls and expensive art fills every corner. There's no warmth, no comfort. Only curated opulence.

Father's voice slices through the room before I can even sit. "Zorina. Finally done playing little concerts?"

Vadim Morozov sits like a king on his throne-like chair, jaw hard, cold eyes sweeping over me like an asset that failed to appreciate in value.

"It wasn't little, Father," I reply tightly, lowering myself onto the stiff settee. "Sold out. National press. My album debuted at number one last month."

His scoff is sharper than any slap. "And yet, you've delayed your marriage. Your duty. That's what happens when women are given too much freedom—they forget their place."

Heat burns under my skin, a dull ache in my chest, but I smile tightly. Misha signed me. Misha made me someone. Not you.

Ivan and Alexei lounge on the other side of the room, talking in low voices about shipments, security runs, power plays. Their conversation carries on like I'm not here. I'm decoration, just another Morozov trophy to be traded for political gain.

Ivan's the elder—brash, cruel in the way oldest sons are allowed to be. Scar on his cheek from a street brawl gone wrong. Alexei's quieter, sharper eyes, but the same dismissive smirk when his gaze flickers over me. Neither bothers to acknowledge my existence beyond my worth as a bargaining chip.

"Maybe you'll finally come to your senses after the wedding," My dad says, swirling his cognac. "No more traveling. No more childish dreams. Misha will set you straight."

My fingers curl against my thigh. My pulse thuds painfully under the diamond band on my finger.

I excuse myself before my anger turns visible. No one stops me. They rarely do.

Upstairs, my room feels like someone else's—a designer's project more than a home. Perfectly arranged, lifeless, untouched except for my violin in the corner. I glance at it but I'm too wrung out to play. My chest is too tight.

I collapse onto the plush mattress, reaching for my phone.

Victor's name lights up the screen before I can even exhale.

VICTOR: *Saw the photos from tonight. You looked like a goddess.*

VICTOR: *Bet Misha didn't even tell you how beautiful you were.*

VICTOR: *I would have.*

I swallow thickly, shame already curling in my belly. I shouldn't respond. Misha protects me. Provides for me. But he doesn't... see me as a woman. Not like Victor pretends to.

ME: *You're drunk.*

His reply is immediate.

VICTOR: *Maybe. But drunk enough to be honest. You deserve more than duty, Zori. You deserve affection. You deserve nights where you're the priority. Where someone's hands memorize every inch of you.*

My thighs press together instinctively, my cheeks flushing with guilt and hunger in equal measure.

I stare at Misha's ring on my finger. Heavy. Cold. Binding.

Victor tempts me with what I crave and what I fear I'll never have.

His last message comes after a pause, brutal in its simplicity.

VICTOR: *Let me give you one real night. Before you trade yourself away.*

My fingers tremble over the screen.

My heart screams no, but my loneliness... my ache... whispers yes.

ME: *Maybe.*

It's a betrayal in one word, but it feels like breathing for the first time.

I hate how stifling it feels to be a Morozova. I doubt it'll be any better once I'm an Antonova. I'll have even less freedom than I do now. Less love, too.

I don't want to betray Mikhail... but I'm not his wife yet. I'm still Zorina Morozova, still single despite my father having promised me to Mikhail. The agreement is informal, and things could change any time based on business and their deal. After all, until recently, the Antonovs and Morozovs used to be sworn enemies.

Things started to shift when the current pakhan, Leo Antonov, took over after his father's death. He expanded the business into legal avenues, grew the Antonov empire into a behemoth worth millions. With his brothers by his side, he acquired businesses and territories until my family was no longer real competition. We're smaller in size, still shackled to the bloody world of illegal drugs.

Leo made an offer my father couldn't refuse—merge our dwindling territory with the Antonov drug empire, which is at least ten times bigger. The price for peace was steep.

But my father didn't pay it.

I did.

By being thrown away like a bargaining chip—a daughter he never wanted.

Rage bites into me, sharp and infuriating. My chest feels tight, my heart heavier than it should at twenty-four. My pussy throbs—not with arousal, but with years of neglect, years of denial. I deserve to live as a woman, to do the things other girls my age do. To be touched, to be desired, to have stories that are mine.

It's not like I didn't try.

I remember one of the rare nights Mikhail lingered after dinner, leaning back in his chair while sipping cognac, gray eyes watchful. I was feeling bold, maybe even reckless, when I asked him, "What if I fall in love with someone else before the wedding?"

His expression didn't even twitch. "You're young, Zorina. Infatuation is natural. I won't fault you for your heart wandering before marriage."

I blinked, stunned, hopeful. "So... if I liked someone else... if I wanted to..."

His eyes cut to mine, glinting steel. "You're free to have harmless crushes. Puppy love. You can look—until you're mine. Once that ring is on your hand in church, your eyes belong to me. Your body belongs to me. Every fucking part of you will belong to me."

I'm snapped back into the present by the chime of another text.

VICTOR: *Did "maybe" mean I have a chance?*

I bite my lip, considering. I'm tired of begging for men's attention. Victor is giving me his attention freely, so why shouldn't I take an offer from the one man who actually wants me?

My fingers hesitate before tapping out a reply.

ME: *Yes.*

His response is almost immediate, a flurry of boldness.

VICTOR: *Thursday night. The Rosewood Presidential Suite at The Cosmopolitan. Eight o'clock.*

ME: *I'm not... looking to just get laid, Victor.*

ME: *I want to be wined and dined. Talked to. Listened to. I want to feel like a woman, not a product, not a trophy.*

When I dreamed of being a musician, but I also dreamed of the lifestyle that would come along with it: a lifestyle of sexual freedom, meeting different kinds of people all over the world, maybe even sleeping with foreign men who caught my eye during my tours. Of course, I could never do that given that Mikhail's men watch me like hawks all the time.

I used to think that meant he wanted me. But he told me he doesn't care who I fall in love with and what I do before our wedding. Sure, that was years ago, when I was nineteen, but he never said things had changed.

Every time I touch Mikhail, he pulls away like I've scalded him. I don't even know if he's interested in me sexually.

I'm pulled away from my thoughts by another text from Victor.

VICTOR: *It'll be my privilege to give you a real night, Zori. No expectations. No pressure. Just you, me, good food, good wine, and good company.*

I chew on my lip, staring at the screen. The words feel nice. Too nice. But there's always that tug in my stomach—a warning. I know Victor. I know his type. Men don't chase women like me for conversation. They all want my body, my pussy, my sexual submission—unless their name happens to be Mikhail Antonov.

ME: *You sure you're not just obsessed with having sex with me?*

ME: *Be honest, Victor.*

His answer takes a little longer this time.

VICTOR: *You are... stunning, Zori. Of course I want you.*

VICTOR: *But I've seen you sad more often than happy. That's what's stuck with me. I want to make that sadness go away. Even if it's just for a little while.*

I blink rapidly, swallowing down the lump in my throat.

No one... no one ever notices that.

My worth is in my obedience, my discipline, my performances. I'm either a violin prodigy or a future Bratva wife. I'm never a person.

Not once has anyone asked how I feel.

It's intoxicating, the idea of being seen.

ME: *I'll be there.*

VICTOR: *Dress sexy for me, sweetheart.*

I roll over onto my stomach, hugging a pillow to my chest. There's something wickedly addictive about knowing I can make a man burn with just the promise of my presence. That my body, my femininity, has power. That I don't have to settle for being invisible anymore.

Minutes later, my phone vibrates again.

MISHA: *Did you get home safely?*

A sharp tug in my chest.

ME: *Yes.*

MISHA: *Did you eat dinner?*

I hesitate. I haven't eaten since lunchtime, nerves and exhaustion settling too heavy in my belly.

ME: No. I was busy. The cook left plenty though.

MISHA: *Go eat something now. Text me when you're done.*

ME: *I will. I promise.*

MISHA: *Sleep well. I'll see you Tuesday. Van Luxor's. Noon sharp.*

ME: *Okay. Goodnight, Misha.*

I stare at our brief exchange, the strange sense of warmth blooming low in my belly. It's not romantic. It's not even sweet.

But it's... consistent. Misha cares in his own way. Quiet. Protective. Respectful. Distant, but constant. It's better than what the cold indifference and sexism mother gets from my father, but it's not what I dream of.

My fingers tighten around my phone.

I did the right thing, I remind myself. This time, I chose me. My needs. My wants.

I force the guilt down and let myself imagine Thursday. The feel of silky sheets, someone's hands lingering on me, being wanted without duty chaining me down.

For once, I'll know what it's like to be Zorina, the woman— not Zorina, the violinist, the daughter.

And I refuse to apologize for it.

FOUR

Misha

I TAKE MY ESPRESSO BLACK, scalding hot, the way I like my mornings—quiet, brutal, and efficient.

But today... it's loud.

Footsteps thunder across the marble flooring of the Antonov estate, heavy bass from some godawful playlist shakes the glass walls, and Nikolai strolls into the kitchen like the smug, overgrown child he is, shirtless and yawning, hair a fucking disaster.

I don't look up from my espresso as I fold my cuffs, sliding the platinum cufflinks through the crisp fabric of my shirt. Dark navy—formal but not flashy. Clean lines, sharp tailoring, nothing inviting. The image of control.

Out of the corner of my eye, I see Nikolai's stupid grin spread. I know it's coming before he opens his mouth.

"Van Luxor's opens at ten," he drawls, plopping into a stool and eyeing my watch. "You're early, brother. Trying to beat the other whipped fiancés?"

I don't flinch, don't smile. I have no idea how he knows my schedule for today, but if he knows, it means my other brothers also know. I down the last of my espresso, the bitter burn a balm for the sharp edge in my chest. "Keep running your mouth, Kolya, and you'll be eating your next meal through a straw."

He throws his head back and laughs like I just made his morning. "Christ, you've got it bad. You used to crush throats for a living, now you're out shopping for diamonds."

Nikolai just grins, unbothered. That's how it's always been with him—youngest Antonov, cocky, charming, too reckless. He spends most of his time womanizing, making jokes, and pretending he's untouchable. He's not. None of us are. Since he got kicked out of school for drinking on campus, he has been bumming around at my house. I've become his de facto 'dad'. He'll soon be going to a boarding school in England, though. In a week, in fact. I wonder if he'll be so carefree there.

Leo, the eldest brother in the family, enters next—black-on-black as usual, pistol tucked under his waistband, a slab of muscle with sharp blue eyes that see everything and reveal nothing. He doesn't need to announce himself; the room adjusts when Leo walks in. *Pakhan*. Boss of the Antonov Bratva. Silent, calculating, deadly. His approval is the currency we all chase, even if none of us admit it.

Aleksei follows, brute force in human form, taller than me, broader too, thick arms covered in ink, knuckles still healing from yesterday's enforcement run. He runs the Bratva's muscle —every piece of territory we own is protected because of Aleksei's ruthlessness. No one crosses him and lives to tell the story. He's completely different when he's with his wife, Lena and their daughter. Lena's pregnant again, and the only reason he's not glued to her side is because she insisted on spending time alone with their daughter and her brother from the orphanage she grew up in. He now works for us. But today is his day off, and he wanted to spend it with his 'niece'.

Dmitry's already at the dining table, laptop open, glasses perched on a sharp nose. Always two steps ahead with numbers, investments, laundering operations. He's the financial brain of the family, turning dirty money clean and expanding our legitimate empire with ice-cold precision. He doesn't lift his head, just mutters, "Van Luxor's opens in an hour."

"I'm not shopping," I say, grabbing my suit jacket from the back of the chair. "I'm investing."

Leo appears in the doorway, silent as ever, arms crossed over his chest, eyes steely and amused. He's dressed down—black slacks, black tee, concealed weapon under his waistband. Always watching. Always calculating.

"For the empire or for the girl?" Leo asks, one brow lifting.

I slide my watch onto my wrist, not answering. Because the answer is messy. Zorina is both—an asset and a weakness. A symbol of peace with Vadim Morozov and the woman who's been haunting my nights. So many times, I've come close to touching her, kissing her, claiming her. But whatever shred of honor I have left pulled me back. Zorina was just a girl, so young when she was engaged to me. I knew I couldn't ruin her youth by touching her, but exposing her to by dark and depraved desires. But once she becomes my wife, there will be no escaping her. She's older now, and that means my excuses for staying away from her are shrinking.

Dmitry doesn't look up when he speaks. "The shares of Stars Entertainment jumped six percent after her last concert. You might want to buy her two diamond sets."

"Maybe three," Aleksei grunts. He grabs a protein shake

from the fridge, cracking his neck. "Keep her occupied so she doesn't realize she's marrying a cold bastard."

The jab is light, but something twists in my chest. I tighten the buttons of my jacket and head toward the door.

Leo's voice follows. "You're taking her to the engagement dinner on Saturday."

"I know," I grunt.

"And the Pakhan expects his second-in-command to at least pretend he's not emotionally constipated," Dmitry adds, without glancing up.

"I can pretend," I clip out. "I've been pretending my entire life."

They go quiet. A rare thing in this household.

For a second, the air feels heavier. Like all of them remember.

Rolan's laugh—loud and reckless—echoes in my head, a ghost I can't exorcise. The photo I keep hidden in my pocket weighs me down like an anchor.

I see it all over again—blood on marble floors, trust shattered under betrayal, the way my cousin's body crumpled because I trusted the wrong man.

I brush the edge of the scar on my palm with my thumb. A permanent reminder. Lesson learned in the most brutal way possible: emotions make you sloppy. Feelings get you killed. And betrayers deserve no mercy.

Rolan has been dead for eight years now, and the guilt still carves me open every day.

A betrayal that I didn't see coming. A friend we trusted sold us out, ambushed us in broad daylight. Rolan bled out because of me. I've worn the scar on my palm since that day, a reminder carved into flesh.

"I'm not falling for her," I mutter, mostly to myself.

My shoulders lock up, muscles coiling tight beneath the tailored fabric.

I turn back toward the door.

"Try not to look like you're attending a funeral," Nikolai calls after me. "She's hot and talented. You're rich and lonely. It's not that complicated."

I pause, glance back, letting my mouth curl into a grin sharp enough to cut. "If you ever talk about my woman like that again, Kolya, you'll be attending your own funeral."

Leo snorts. Aleksei laughs. Dmitry just keeps typing.

I adjust my cuffs one last time and step outside into the sun, letting the steel armor of duty settle over me.

Van Luxor's awaits.

So does Zorina.

And this time, maybe I won't be able to walk away without touching her, even if it's platonically.

VAN LUXOR'S is more than a jewelry store—it's a fortress of indulgence. Polished marble floors gleam under chandeliers worth millions, gold-trimmed mirrors line the walls, and every piece of jewelry is nestled in velvet so plush it could make a sultan weep. Private rooms for VIP clients—like me—are tucked in the back, where no one asks questions about how money is made, only how much of it you're willing to spend.

But none of it touches me.

Not today.

Because when Zorina walks through those double doors, my throat locks up.

She's late, and I should be irritated—scratch that, I am—but one look at her and my irritation turns into something far darker.

She's wrapped in some delicate slip dress, the color of pale champagne, clinging to every dangerous curve of her body. Thin straps slide off one shoulder, silky fabric caressing her hips, teasing the shape of her thighs with every step she takes. Her hair falls in those long, soft waves down her back, and her full lips are stained pink, just enough to make a man imagine sinful things.

My body reacts immediately, tightening in places it shouldn't in public, heat coiling low and fast. I force my jaw to lock and remind myself of the vow I made: hands off until after the wedding. After the contract is sealed. After she's mine in name, not just on paper.

But fuck—she makes that vow feel like a noose around my neck.

"Sorry I'm late," she murmurs, soft, almost shy, eyes glancing down at the floor like she's afraid to meet my stare.

Meek. Quiet. Submissive.

It just pisses me off. Where the hell is her fire?

When we settle into the private suite, the manager approaches, dripping with pleasantries. I wave him off with a nod. "Bring out the bridal collections. The after-party pieces too."

"Of course, Mr. Antonov." He scurries off, leaving us alone with a view of the Strip's glittering skyline through floor-to-ceiling windows.

Zorina perches on the velvet stool, all grace and elegance, but I see the tension in her spine. The way she refuses to meet my eyes. The way her fingers keep brushing her ring like she's reminding herself it's there.

"Something funny on your phone?" I ask quietly.

Her head snaps up, eyes wide. "No."

Lie.

The worst part? She's terrible at lying. The little flush creeping up her chest gives her away.

I lean forward, resting my hands on the table, letting my body fill her space. "You smiled at your phone more than you've ever smiled at me. Care to explain?"

Her throat works, lips parting, but before she can answer, the staff rolls in cart after cart of necklaces, bracelets, and sparkling diamonds.

"Oh, that one looks pretty." She picks up a diamond necklace with sapphires, eyes glittering with pleasure. She grabs onto the distraction like a lifeline, evading my question, which only sharpens my suspicions. Why is she trying to avoid answering me?

She tries on the necklace with the staff's help, then shakes her head. "This won't match with my outfit."

"You can buy it anyway," I say. "If you like it."

Her eyes widen. It's been six years of me buying her expensive things, and every time, she acts like it's the first time. "No. I can't have you spending so much. We'll pick something else. Something more suitable."

My jaw tightens. Her words are grateful, but there's something hollow underneath. Something... resigned. She slides her phone out of her purse, looking at the screen. When she sees no new message notifications, the disappointment on her face is palpable. Who the hell is she waiting for messages from? A lover? A friend? Her brothers?

My teeth grind. I didn't bring her here for fucking gratitude. I didn't bring her here because I had to. But I hate that she's distracted by something and I don't even know what. I could ask her, but I don't want to. I want her to tell me her secrets willingly, to show me that she trusts me.

Yet, anger and helplessness surges through me like a wave,

rising high, fast. I lean over, plucking a diamond choker from the nearest case, and step behind her.

Her body freezes.

Good.

The cool platinum catches the light as I brush her hair over one shoulder, fingers skimming the nape of her neck. Her breath catches, skin pebbling beneath my touch.

"Lift your chin," I murmur.

She obeys, swallowing hard, her throat so delicate I have the sudden, violent urge to mark it.

My fingers work the clasp, the chain settling around her slender neck, the diamond pendant falling right above the soft curve of her breasts.

She shudders when my knuckles graze the tops of her breasts, her pulse fluttering wildly under my fingertips.

I lean down, lips dangerously close to her ear, enough for her to feel my breath ghost along her skin. "This looks good on you."

Her eyes flutter shut, lips parting with a soft, involuntary gasp.

Possession roars in my chest. Mine.

I stare at her through the mirror's reflection—gold and diamonds hugging the delicate curve of her throat, her posture regal, her profile stunning. She looks like she was born for this life. Like a queen, poised and cold... except for the way her fingers twitch, her chest rises and falls just a touch too quickly, and when our eyes lock, I see the quiet chaos she tries to hide.

I lean in, voice a low growl. "I'd like to take this off you... on our wedding night."

Her breath stutters. Color rushes up her cheeks, softening her usual sharp edges, making her look younger... sweeter. Tempting. Beautiful and soft in a way that makes every possessive instinct in me tighten.

I shouldn't. I know I shouldn't.

But I let myself go further than I ever have.

I press a kiss to her shoulder, letting my lips linger against the silky fabric of her dress, letting her feel my mouth there, marking her, branding her in my own way.

Zorina turns her head slightly, just enough for her gaze to meet mine from under thick lashes, cheeks still warm, lips parted. "We should get this one... since you like it."

My chest tightens.

I tilt my head, studying her expression. "Do you like it?"

Her smile doesn't reach her eyes. "That's never mattered. It won't matter now. You're the one paying."

Her tone is light but sharp, laced with something bitter beneath the softness. A quiet, strangled anger she thinks I won't notice.

But I do.

I should remind her not to talk back. Should reprimand her for that tone—every woman before her would've been punished for less. But I can't do it. Not today. Something is... off. Different.

I smooth my palm down the silk at her lower back, a gentle sweep meant to soothe. "We can choose something else. Something you like."

Her jaw tightens, her fingers tracing the gold around her throat absentmindedly. "I'd rather go home."

There it is. The crack beneath the polished surface. The distance widening between us without warning. I don't know why. But I'm not stupid. It started after those texts she keeps smiling at. The ones she's trying to hide from me.

I make a note to have Viktor find out who it is, but for now, I say nothing. I can't afford to push her further away.

I wave the store assistant over, my voice hardening. "We'll take this necklace. And the matching earrings."

The man nods eagerly and disappears to box up the purchase.

Zorina pulls out her phone again, thumbs flying across the screen. My jaw ticks.

I step into her space, sliding an arm firmly around her waist, my fingers splaying against her hip possessively. "You're not going home yet."

Her head snaps up, startled. "What?"

I lean down, my lips brushing against the shell of her ear, my breath hot and sure. "We're having dinner. A date."

Her brows knit, confusion clouding those big, pretty eyes. "You never—"

"Now I am," I cut her off smoothly, steering her toward the exit, palm pressing firmly to her lower back, staking my claim as we leave. "Let's go, little dove."

She swallows, hesitating for a split second before following my lead.

Good. Let her text whoever she wants.

By for the next few hours... she'll only think of me.

FIVE

Zorina

VICTOR'S TEXTS keep pinging on my phone like little sparks, flaring with romantic one-liners and ridiculously cheesy compliments.

If anyone else texted me things like, *"You deserve to be kissed breathless under the stars,"* I'd laugh and block them. But with Victor... I don't know. I don't laugh. I read every message twice, sometimes three times, letting the words soak into the cracks inside me. They make me feel wanted—like a teenage girl who is getting attention from a boy for the first time.

It's intoxicating.

Even if they're cliché, even if I know they're meaningless promises from a man who wants what he's never had... it feels good to be wanted like this.

But I can't respond. Not with Mikhail Antonov sitting directly opposite me, his steely gray gaze cutting across the table like a blade.

I flick my phone face down, pressing it against my thigh, hiding it under the tablecloth.

He's too damn perceptive.

And God help me... too damn handsome.

Broad shoulders strain against the sharp cut of his black tailored suit. His shirt, open at the collar, reveals a glimpse of bronze skin and the thick column of his throat. His hair is dark brown, neatly slicked back today, and those sharp cheekbones—carved like sin—could slice through glass. But it's the mouth that undoes me. Straight, unsmiling, cruelly perfect. Except when it softens... like earlier today. When he kissed me on the shoulder. It made my entire body glow like someone had lit a fire inside me. For a second, I was alive, anticipating more. Wanting him to go further, to kiss my breasts, my hard nipples, and every exposed inch of my body.

My thighs shift restlessly.

I shouldn't be reacting to him. I shouldn't be remembering the way his lips pressed to my shoulder, the rough whisper in my ear about our wedding night, the raw possessiveness burning in his eyes when he told me he wanted to take the necklace off me himself.

That moment shouldn't make my core clench. But it does.

Maybe... maybe sleeping with Misha won't be as bad as I feared.

Maybe I won't be left unsatisfied in some ice-cold marriage bed. Maybe, just maybe, he'll take me with the same feral hunger I glimpsed in his gaze today.

I curl my toes inside my stilettos, pressing my knees together beneath the table, hating myself a little for even thinking this way.

I'm nurturing hopes that will only be dashed later. I have been in the bratva long enough to know that most men in the bratva make love the same way they do everything else—coldly and efficiently. My own mother has never experienced an orgasm and neither have my brothers' wives. They were just wombs to bear children. They pleasure, their fulfillment wasn't even an afterthought. Men in the bratva are old-fashioned in all the wrong ways.

I want to believe that Mikhail will be different. That he will try to make things good for me. But I'm scared I'll be disillusioned. He's even less emotional than my brothers. I've never seen him get angry or show any intense emotions. He's always controlled, his voice even and calm.

"Malyshka." His low, gravelly voice cuts through my thoughts. "You're distracted."

I blink, lifting my head and straightening my spine. "Just thinking."

His gray eyes sharpen. "About?"

I set my jaw, fingers curling around my glass of sparkling water. "If I'd have had a better life as a normal girl."

Something flickers in his gaze. His broad chest shifts as he leans back in his chair, fingers tapping rhythmically against the table.

"If I were a normal girl, I could do whatever I wanted, be with whoever I wanted. I would live in a different world, one where the bratva doesn't exist. If I were a normal girl, you could have married someone else. Someone more beautiful or I don't know...quieter. You'd be married already, instead of waiting for me to live out my dreams."

His jaw ticks, and there's a flash of irritation in his eyes. "It doesn't matter to me. I don't want to marry someone else."

My eyebrows arch. "Because all women are the same to you?"

His lips twitch, the barest hint of amusement. "No. Because you're the one destined for me."

I stare at him. My heart tightens, but not in a good way.

Not in a way that makes me feel special. I grit my teeth, my smile strained. "So... fate. No choice."

"It's still destiny, even if you're a normal girl and happen to meet the love of your life in a café," he says smoothly. "Doesn't matter if it's forged through business or born in chance. Some people are meant to be together."

I want to scream at how calmly he says it. Like it's already decided, no matter what I feel.

"So..." I swallow. "If I asked to break off the engagement, would you let me go? Consider that fate, too?"

His expression hardens immediately. "Are you planning to break it off?"

Shit. Panic flares in my chest. My tongue trips over itself. "No! Just... marriage nerves. That's all. I didn't mean that."

He doesn't believe me. I can see it in his narrowed gaze, the way he goes eerily still.

"What kind of man would you have married... if you'd had a choice?" His voice is low, almost... careful.

I shrug, masking the ache in my chest. "Someone who loves me. Who... romances me. Looks at me like I matter more than anything else in the world. Wants to spend all his free time with me, talking about nothing and everything. Who touches me and shows affection."

Silence stretches between us, heavy and suffocating.

His jaw flexes once before he leans in, voice curt. "I'll give you anything you want after we marry. Money. Staff. Security. You won't have to lift a finger if you don't want to. My staff will take care of you."

So much control. So much suffocation wrapped in a neat little package. So much of everything I don't want, even if it's exactly what other girls dream of.

"And kids?" I ask quietly.

His brow furrows. "I haven't thought about it."

Liar. With four brothers, raised in a dynasty of power, he's definitely thought about it. He just doesn't want to admit it.

I imagine little boys with steely eyes and sharp cheekbones, little girls with violins tucked beneath their arms. A big family where I can finally feel like I belong. Loved.

It relaxes my muscles, soothes something frayed and broken inside me. I've always wanted to hold my own babies, to feel the warmth of a tiny heartbeat fluttering beneath my skin, to cradle life that is mine, born from me. Not an obligation. Something I chose to create, chose to nurture. Just... mine.

I imagine pressing kisses to soft little cheeks, breathing in the innocent scent of my babies. I'd tell them every single day how much I love them, how proud they make me, how nothing in the world is more precious than them. I wouldn't have to fake smiles or watch my words like I do with men. Children love freely. They wouldn't punish me for speaking my mind or shame me for wanting attention. They would wrap their tiny fingers around mine and hold on tight, needing me in the way I've always needed someone.

And Mikhail... the image hits me so hard it knocks the breath out of me.

Mikhail standing behind me, his big, protective hands splayed over my swollen stomach. Possessively stroking my body like he owns it, knowing he knocked me up and being proud of it. Mikhail bending low to kiss my stretched skin, murmuring in Russian to the baby growing inside me. His sharp gray eyes softening when he feels a kick under his palm. I press my thighs together as my nerves tingle in places I didn't expect.

I want that. God, I want it so badly my chest aches.

Maybe I'll never have Mikhail's love... but I'll have his children. And maybe that will be enough.

A warm flush rises on my cheeks just as Mikhail's deep

voice rumbles across the table. "What were you thinking just now?"

I jerk in my seat, blinking rapidly. "Nothing."

His mouth kicks up in a knowing smirk, but he lets it go.

The waiter arrives, and Mikhail, without hesitation, orders for me like always. "She'll have the seared salmon, no capers, with the truffle risotto—"

"Actually," I cut in smoothly, lifting my chin. "I'd prefer the filet mignon, medium rare, with garlic butter sauce... and the crispy roasted potatoes."

The waiter hesitates, eyes darting between us like a rabbit caught between two wolves.

Mikhail's jaw clenches. His eyes narrow like steel doors slamming shut... before he gives a slight nod. "Make it as she said."

The waiter scurries off and I stare across the table, daring Mikhail to say something.

His eyes glint. "Testing limits now, are we?"

"Just letting you know I have preferences," I answer sweetly.

"I know you do, malyshka. You've never been good at hiding them."

"I didn't know I was supposed to," I shoot back, pushing my water glass away.

His mouth twitches, that cold amusement dancing at the edges of his lips. "Keep going like this, and you'll have me thinking you enjoy disobedience."

"Maybe I do," I murmur, defiant even though my pulse is racing.

His eyes darken, but before he can reply, the waiter returns with bread, breaking the tension. We eat in silence after that, like always. The usual heavy, suffocating quiet stretching between us, making my heart sink. No laughter. No teasing. Just the quiet clink of cutlery and unsaid words.

So much for ever having the kind of marriage where we actually talk.

By the time we step out of the restaurant, the air is crisp and cool, but the tension coils hotter between us. I reach for my phone, my fingers itching for validation, for the little thrill Victor's messages give me.

Another text flashes on my screen.

Victor: I'll pick you up Thursday night, princess. Can't wait to touch you and make you scream.

A tiny smile creeps across my lips before I can stop it.

And then I'm spinning.

Mikhail's palm hits my lower back, pressing me back, my spine slamming into the brick wall of the alley. His body crowds mine, his hard chest pressing into my softer curves, heat radiating off him like a furnace.

He growls. Actually growls like he's a feral wolf or something. There's a dangerous emotion glinting in his eyes as he says, "I don't like when you're distracted."

His lips crash down on mine before I can take a breath.

It's not sweet or gentle.

It's brutal. Possessive. Punishing.

His mouth takes and takes, tongue pushing between my lips, claiming my mouth with raw, vicious hunger. My hands fly up to clutch at his jacket, my back arching into him as his thigh presses between mine. Every kiss, every lash of his tongue, every scrape of his teeth feels like I'm being set on fire from the inside out.

When his teeth sink into my bottom lip, tugging it sharply, I gasp, my legs threatening to give out. I'm wrecked, panting, dizzy. By the time he pulls back, my lips are swollen, slick, and I'm pretty sure my panties are ruined.

His thumb brushes along my cheekbone, and he growls low in my ear, "Is that enough romance for you?"

I can't answer. My throat feels tight, my mouth wrecked from his brutal kiss.

"And another thing," he says darkly. "I don't like it when you look elsewhere. You're supposed to be looking at me. Remember that."

With that, he steps back, adjusting his suit like nothing happened, his expression schooled back into cold indifference.

But me?

I'm standing against the wall, pulse hammering, lips bruised, body shaking... and I have no idea which man is more dangerous—Victor with his sweet promises or Mikhail with his punishing kisses.

Maybe I'll never survive either of them.

SIX

Zorina

THE GLOSSY MARBLE floors of the Rosewood Hotel glisten under the chandeliers, each step of my stilettos clicking against the polished surface like a countdown to regret.

Victor's hand rests a little too low on my back, his fingertips grazing the curve of my ass as he steers me through the grand lobby. I stiffen, spine rigid beneath the clinging silk of my dress. A deep red number with thin straps and a plunging neckline that hugs my waist and frames my breasts in a way that always makes men's gazes dip—and tonight, Victor's eyes haven't strayed from my chest since I stepped out of the car.

I swallow the bitter lump forming in my throat.

This was a mistake.

I knew it the second I caught the gleam of hunger in Victor's gaze, the second his smile stretched too wide, his hand too familiar. His texts had been... charming, in their desperate, clumsy way. Whispered promises of romantic dinners, long walks, someone who would actually listen to me, touch me with affection instead of obligation.

But now? Now, I feel like prey. Like meat on a silver platter, and Victor is ready to sink his teeth in.

"Mmm," Victor hums approvingly, his lips grazing my temple. "You look absolutely fuckable tonight, princess."

My stomach churns. Even when Mikhail was angry—possessive to the point of madness—he never made me feel unsafe. Never made my skin crawl. Even when his grip bruised my waist, when his mouth devoured mine, I felt... protected. I felt like my body was shielded inside his arms, like I could relax because my subconscious knew he would never let anyone else touch me or harm me.

But with Victor, there's no sense of safety, no sense of trust or reassurance. His passion is so different from Misha's—there's no honor, no self-restraint. And even though I've hated my fiancé's self-controlled nature, I now realize there are things worse than a man who doesn't act on his urges.

Victor's hand dips lower, fingers squeezing. My jaw tightens.

"Where are we going?" I ask, forcing lightness into my tone. "You promised me dinner. I thought we'd start with food."

Victor chuckles, his grin oily, his hand producing a sleek black keycard. "We're headed straight to the suite, baby. I thought we could order room service later... after you've worked up an appetite."

My throat closes.

God, I was so fucking naive.

Of course he wasn't interested in talking. Of course all those texts were just bait to get me here, half-naked, eager to be wanted.

A surge of shame crashes into me.

No. No, I'm not doing this.

But before I can twist away, the elevator doors slide open—cool, metallic panels revealing a broad chest wrapped in an immaculately tailored charcoal suit.

My heart flatlines.

Mikhail.

Towering. Lethal. Wolf-like.

His brown hair is slicked back, strands gleaming beneath the elevator's soft lighting. His sharp cheekbones are cut from stone, his brutal mouth unsmiling. And his eyes—those steely gray irises lock onto me, then lower to Victor's hand on my ass, and then darken into a storm of pure, unfiltered rage.

I shiver, goosebumps prickling across my exposed skin.

"Mikhail," Victor stammers, trying to recover, his voice suddenly unsure. "What a—uh—surprise."

Mikhail doesn't blink. His whole body radiates restrained violence, his jaw ticking, his hands fisting at his sides before his voice rolls out, lethal and low.

"Unhand my wife."

Victor swallows, his hand twitching but not moving away. "Technically, she's not your wife yet—"

Mikhail moves.

One moment Victor is standing smugly beside me, the next Mikhail has him pinned against the golden elevator frame, one large hand wrapped around his throat, squeezing. Victor's feet scramble against the marble.

"I won't repeat myself," Mikhail growls, squeezing harder.

Victor gasps, releasing me instantly, his face turning crimson.

"Mikhail!" I hiss, tugging at his sleeve, panic tightening my chest. "Security—someone's going to call security."

His cold laughter is like knives dancing along my spine. "No one will throw me out of my own fucking hotel."

Victor chokes, his eyes bulging.

Mikhail's free hand fishes out his phone, typing a few commands before speaking into it. "Oleg, come to the lobby. Escort Victor Kovalenko out of the premises. He's banned from every Antonov-owned property."

Victor makes a strangled noise of protest, his feet kicking.

"And cancel his contract with Stars Entertainment," Mikhail adds without looking at me. "He's no longer associated with my fiancée."

Victor's head jerks. "Y-you can't— I'm a guest— I have the presidential suite—"

Mikhail grins, a sharp glint in his gray eyes as he plucks the keycard from Victor's jacket pocket. "Not anymore. Now it's mine."

My pulse races as Mikhail steps back, brushing off his sleeves like Victor's existence left filth behind.

Two men in sleek black suits appear from nowhere, Oleg included, gripping Victor by the arms. He tries to bark threats, but Mikhail doesn't even glance his way.

Mikhail's gaze slices through the space where Victor used to stand, leaving me breathless and shaky. As the two men in suits drag Victor away, I can still feel the heat radiating from Mikhail's body, the raw power that thrums through him like an electric current.

"Mikhail," I whisper, but the word gets swallowed by the weight of the tension hanging between us. He turns, those stormy eyes locking onto mine with a fierce intensity that makes my heart race and my stomach churn.

"Step into the elevator," he commands, his voice low and unyielding. There's no room for argument. My feet move before I can think too hard about it, following him as if drawn by an invisible string.

The door slides shut behind us, sealing us in this confined space. I lean against the cool metal wall, trying to catch my breath as Mikhail stands before me, arms crossed and jaw set like granite.

I'm still reeling from the adrenaline of what just happened, my heart racing as I step into the elevator. Mikhail's presence fills the small space, eclipsing everything else around me. The tension is electric, thick with unspoken words and unresolved feelings.

He stands tall, his broad shoulders filling the cabin like a looming storm, and I can feel his anger radiating off him in waves. His eyes narrow as they scan my body, lingering far too long on the way my dress clings to my curves, how the fabric accentuates my breasts and leaves little to the imagination.

"Did you come here to whore yourself out to a man like Victor?" he growls, his voice low and dangerous.

I recoil slightly at his words, but I refuse to let him see that I'm shaken. "That's not true," I snap back, my voice trembling but firm.

His jaw tightens, a muscle ticking in his cheek.

"If that's not the case," Mikhail snarls, taking a step closer, "then why are you dressed like a hooker? With your tits out on display like you're begging for a man's touch?"

His words hit me like a slap, but I refuse to cower. Instead, I straighten my spine, meeting his furious gaze.

"Because I wanted to feel wanted!" The words burst from me, raw and honest. "I wanted one night of being desired before I marry a man who treats me like a business contract. You never touch me, never look at me. What was I supposed to do?"

His eyes narrow dangerously. "So you thought you'd spread your legs for the first man who seduced you?"

"You told me it was okay," I shoot back, my voice trembling but fiery. "You said it yourself years ago—that I could fall in love with someone else before we married. That you wouldn't fault me for it."

Something shifts in his expression, a dark understanding dawning. In a flash, he's on me, pressing me against the wall of the elevator, one large hand circling my throat. Not squeezing, but holding me in place, his thumb resting against my racing pulse.

"I told you," he rasps, his voice venom-laced steel, "you can be infatuated with other men. You can have your little crushes. But I never—ever—said you could let another man put his hands on you."

My skin prickles. My thighs tremble, betraying me. I can't breathe, not from his grip but from the intensity rolling off him in waves. My knees weaken, a shameful heat pooling between my thighs. My pussy throbs like a slut, begging to be filled, to be stretched by his brutal fingers and cock.

"I'll make sure you remember that in the future," he promises, his voice like gravel.

The elevator continues its smooth ascent, and I manage to whisper, "Where are we going?"

His free hand trails up my collarbone, fingertips skimming over my exposed skin, tracing the swell of my breast above the neckline of my dress. I shiver uncontrollably, a soft gasp escaping my lips.

His laugh is low and sinister, a sound that makes me tremble with both fear and anticipation.

"To the presidential suite, of course." His eyes darken as they hold mine. "If you want to lose your virginity so badly, malyshka, I'll help you."

My heart hammers against my ribs, my body responding to his words with embarrassing eagerness. I should be angry. I should push him away. But God help me, I can't.

"I don't understand," I whisper, my voice barely audible. "You never wanted me before."

His hand tightens slightly around my throat, tilting my

head back. "You understand nothing, little one. I've wanted you since the first moment I saw you. But unlike that pathetic excuse for a man downstairs, I know how to control myself."

My knees nearly buckle.

God help me—I should feel angry, afraid... but all I feel is the heat unfurling in my belly, the wicked thrill of his possessive promise.

And a terrifying realization settles in my chest.

I've been playing with fire.

And tonight, I'm going to get burned.

SEVEN

Mikhail

THE ELEVATOR DINGS, doors sliding open to reveal the final floor. I don't wait for her to step out. I don't wait for her to follow my command. I'm done waiting.

In one fluid motion, I bend down and hoist Zorina's body over my shoulder, her slight weight nothing against my strength. She gasps, the sound transforming into a squeak of indignation as her world tilts upside down.

"Mikhail! Put me down!" Her fists begin to pound against my back, each impact as light as a butterfly's wings against steel. All I feel is her delectable tits, big and firm as they press against my back. Her pebbled nipples are hard enough that I feel them through my white shirt. My cock responds instantly as she presses her hard nubs into my back, digging them deeper into my flesh.

I feel a bolt of electricity slicing through my cock, making it tighten with need.

I ignore her protests, striding down the hallway with purpose, her body draped over my shoulder like a prize. The key card slides into the presidential suite door with a satisfying click.

"I mean it! This is ridiculous—you can't just—"

The door swings open, revealing the sprawling luxury of the hotel's finest accommodation. Floor-to-ceiling windows frame the glittering Las Vegas skyline, the city's neon heartbeat pulsing against the darkening sky. Crystal chandeliers cast golden light across Italian marble floors, illuminating the massive living area with its white leather couches and glass tables adorned with fresh orchids. To the right, a full bar gleams with top-shelf liquor in crystal decanters. Beyond that, double doors lead to a master bedroom with a California king bed draped in Egyptian cotton.

This suite was supposed to be her love nest with Victor tonight. The thought makes my blood boil all over again.

I kick the door shut behind us, the sound echoing through the cavernous space. Zorina's body bounces slightly against my shoulder as she renews her struggles.

"Put me down! This isn't funny anymore!" Her fists beat a little harder now, her legs kicking uselessly in the air.

"Funny?" I growl, my voice dropping to a dangerous register. "You think any of this is funny to me?"

With one swift movement, I deposit her onto the white leather couch. She lands with a soft thud, her red dress riding up her thighs, golden hair spilling around her flushed face. Beautiful. Furious. Mine.

"It's too late for your protests now, Zorina." I stalk toward the bar, pouring myself two fingers of whiskey, letting the amber liquid burn down my throat. "In the bratva, betrayal equals death."

Her eyes widen, genuine fear flickering across her features. Good. She should be afraid.

"I didn't betray you," she whispers, her voice small but defiant. "I wasn't going to...I was about to leave. I swear. I thought he was going to court me properly, but when I realized what Victor really wanted from me, I was ready to go home. But he wouldn't let me."

I slam the glass down hard enough that the crystal cracks in my grip. Blood wells from a small cut on my palm—right next to the old scar, the one I've carried for eight years. The one that reminds me every day what betrayal costs.

And I swore that I'd never again go easy on someone who lies to me and betrays me. Even if it's my sweet, vulnerable fiancée.

"Is that what you tell yourself?" I walk toward her, blood dripping down my knuckles, a dark satisfaction burning cold through the pain. "You were half-naked. You let him put his arm on your hip. You were ready to let him come inside you. Don't insult my intelligence. Or your own."

She clamps her lips together and I can see the panic in her eyes, the barest tremor in her hands. She's afraid—of me, of herself, of what this means. Something about that fear makes me want to ruin her and worship her all at once.

I finish my drink in a single swallow, letting the whiskey set fire to the rage clawing at my insides. I want to hurt her. I want to haul her onto my cock and fuck her until she forgets any man's name but mine. I want to erase every trace of him—no, of any man—from her body and mind. Burn myself into her soul.

It's the oldest story in the world: girl gets too close to the flame, only to learn that the fire has teeth.

She's staring at my hand, eyes wide at the blood, but I ignore it. I unbutton my sleeves, rolling them up with slow, deliberate menace. I want her to see what she's done to me. I want her to know the power she has, and I want to show her what I do to things that belong to me.

I move to her in three strides, yank her up off the couch by her wrist. The delicate bones grind under my grip, but she doesn't flinch. She stares at me, defiant and trembling, lips parted as if she's about to protest—but she doesn't.

I drag her down the hall and into the master bedroom. I don't stop to turn on the lights. The only illumination is the city skyline, neon pinks and bruised purples slashing across the windows, flickering with each pulse of the Vegas night. I throw Zorina onto the bed, her body bouncing twice against the cloud-white linens, her dress bunching around her thighs. The sight makes my cock throb so hard it nearly hurts.

She screams then, more in outrage than fear, hair wild around her face. "You can't just—"

I crawl on top of her in a breath, pinning her wrists over her head with one hand, my bleeding palm smearing crimson across her skin, marking her as I lower my face until our noses brush. "I can. I will. You want to fuck? You want to see what it's like to be broken in by an Antonov? You've got my full attention, princess. Let's get started."

Her breath comes in hot little gasps. Her thighs press together, hips squirming beneath me as I straddle her, my weight pressing her into the mattress.

In the dark, I can see the outline of her breasts, heaving under the thin red silk. My free hand moves to her throat, thumb pressing lightly just under her jaw. Her pulse flutters there—a wild bird, helpless in my grasp. I lean in, lips grazing her earlobe, whispering, "I'm going to pop your cherry tonight. Your virgin blood is going to be all over my hands, soaking into my skin."

My lips crash onto hers, brutal and unyielding. The taste of her, sweet and intoxicating, fuels the fire that's been burning within me for years. I've waited, watched, and now, I'm claiming what's mine.

Her body trembles under my touch, a mix of fear and desire that only makes me harder. She's my little dove, my Malyshka, and tonight, she'll know the depth of my obsession.

I strip her piece by piece, my hands rough and demanding. Her dress falls apart easily under my fingers and I drag it to the floor. Her bare stomach is gorgeous. Soft and slender.

I can smell the fertility radiating off her skin like perfume.

She whimpers, her eyes wide with a mix of shock and longing. "Misha, please...please don't..." Her voice is a plea, a desperate cry for more. I can't resist the urge to give her everything she needs, everything she craves.

My fingers trail down her spine, making her shudder. She's in a small lacy scrap of a bra, barely holding in her beautiful tits, and her longing for me is already leaking through her panties. I unhook her bra, letting it fall away, exposing her pink nipples, hard and ready for my mouth. I groan.

She tries to grab me, but I hold her forearms, stilling her. My tongue brushes her chest, and she shudders underneath me. "For years, you were the one thing I told myself I couldn't have. The one sweet fruit I couldn't bite into. But my hunger for you is far too strong. And tonight, I won't be satisfied until I've buried my cock inside your virgin cunt and claimed you."

Zorina's eyes widen in shock but she stops resisting.

She moans as I suck on her tits, the nipples turning a deeper shade of pink under my attention. Her body writhes as I palm her breasts, marveling at their perfection. "Misha!"

She's begging me, but I'm in no rush. My tongue delves into her mouth, claiming her, tasting her, and the need raging through my veins right now is nothing short of raw starvation.

I feel her thighs arch against my knees. She doesn't know what she wants, but I do: I want to breed her. In my mind's eye,

I can see large and swollen breasts leaking milk for the babies she's going to have. *My* babies.

When I finally pull away, her lips are swollen and red from my kiss. I rip through her underwear, and her breath hitches with shock as she feels the jerk. I toss what remains of the cheap fabric to one side.

I spread her legs apart, greedily devouring her pussy with my eyes. It's slick with arousal, the folds vibrating with need.

"You look so pretty when you're dripping for me." I tease her folds with my fingers, pressing against the softness.

Zorina's legs are spread wide beneath me, her body quivering, that flush deepening on her neck and cheeks. I can smell her pheromones, and I know she's ready for me. Ready and fertile.

I go to my knees and put my tongue on her.

Her thighs clamp around my head. I lick round and round her clit, sucking the little bud into my mouth and fluttering my tongue against it. Each lick makes her whimper, each soft touch makes her cry out. "Oh my god, are you really..." Her words fade as she closes her eyes, surrendering to a wave of pleasure.

I lick every inch of the delicate folds of her pussy, the silken skin slick and wet with her juice. My mouth sucks, my lips pull at her hot little cunt, my tongue slides deep into that tight forbidden channel. I can't taste enough of her. I can't get enough of her sweet juices. I'm greedy and starving. Mad with need.

She bends and writhes under my mouth. My face is drenched, smeared with her cream. She's so wet she gushes on my tongue.

I need to breed her. I need to pump her full of cum and mark her pussy. I'm going to ruin her cunt, make it mine in every way.

I push her thighs apart, holding down her body on the

mattress— fuck she's so wet, so ready— and I'm almost out of control, consumed with the need to fuck her hard and deep, mark her every day, every hour, so no one will forget to which man she belongs.

"Zorina," I hiss, my teeth bared. My whole body shakes, trembles with unrestrained lust. I push my tongue in her, knowing I'm breaching the final walls of her innocence. Her curvy body tenses, tightens around my tongue, and she's moaning, panting, begging me for release. To let her come.

Zorina's head thrashes from side to side, and my eyes are magnetized to her writhing form as she struggles to get closer to my tongue, her cunt weeping from where she pushed up against me. I flick the tip over her clit, and she squeaks out my name. I smile but keep stroking her. She's already sensitive, and her whole body is trembling like a live wire as I tease her clit.

Zorina's dazed blue eyes gleam blindingly at me, and as I suckle on her clit, pulling that red bud into my mouth, her cunt convulses on my tongue. She smells like sex and musk. Like sweet innocence being corrupted.

I lick.

"Misha...Misha...please, oh my God! I—I'm..." She explodes like a beautiful feminine goddess, her hips rocking on my mouth, her cum gushing into my mouth, her thighs wet. My fingers rubbing her clit as she whimpers, her voice broken with each moan. And all she can do is call my name. Again and again.

Because she knows I'm the one who broke her body. Showed her the ultimate pleasure. Gave her the first orgasm of her life.

Something dark and possessive stirs inside me. I'm going to take all her firsts. Her first orgasm, her first time, her first kiss, her first pregnancy...she's going to give me everything she has.

Dominance pushes against my nerves. Pride swells in my

chest at the filthy sounds she makes. Knowing I made her croon like a filthy slut is like a drug injected into my veins.

I drag my palm over her chest, squeezing her breasts.

"Oh, God..." She gasps, arching against me.

"God has nothing to do with us," I growl. I tear off my shirt, buttons pinging on the floor as I rip it open, and then I shove off the rest of my clothes. Her eyes widen when she sees me naked, my cock long and thick, the heavy sac below full of seed.

"Mikhail..." she rasps, as if she's afraid and yet nodding her head slightly up and down as if she knows she's being claimed, owned, and bred. Just the way nature intended.

"What?" I smirk down at her, pushing her thighs further apart, holding them down on the bed with bruising force. "Don't beg me unless you want my cock. Because that's why I'm going to give you. Your pussy is nice and relaxed after that orgasm, isn't it?"

Nervousness flits across her features. But it's gone, replaced by lust and longing.

"What do you want, Zorina?" I ask her mockingly, my voice low and gravelly. "Do you want me to take care of your sweet pussy? Tell me. I love it when you beg."

Her hands fist the bedsheets, thighs trembling. "Please—"

"Please what?" I press two fingers into her, her pussy clenching at me, slick with arousal, preparing for my cock.

"N-no..." she moans. "Please."

"God, you're going to take every inch of my cock like a good little obedient wife even though you're not even one yet," I groan, my fingers circling her pussy again. "I'm going to teach you exactly what being my woman means. Submission. Compliance. And every night, you're going to take my seed inside you because you want my babies, don't you? You're aching to get your womb full of me. I can see it in your eyes."

Her breath hitches, eyes dilating, a soft cry escaping her

parted lips as she feels another wave of pleasure building.

"I'm going to suck your tits dry every morning after I wake up to find you already taking care of our babies. I can already see your nipples swollen and leaking with milk. Those big tits of yours swollen to the point of bursting. You won't be able to walk without feeling my cum dripping out of you; you'll be so full."

I lean over her, sucking her nipples into my mouth, tasting her soft skin, imagining the taste of her milk on my tongue. She quivers, arching into my touch, moaning softly as I nip and suck, pulling her flesh between my teeth.

"You want to be a good little cum-slut for me, don't you?" I groan, suckling on her nipples. My cock is so hard it's aching, precum already spilling onto her belly. "You want me to fill this pussy until you're bursting, to stretch you wide with my cock and breed you raw."

She's moaning incoherently now, hips bucking up to push herself against my hand as I apply even more pressure on her clit, rolling and rubbing it between my two fingers.

I spread her thighs open and press a kiss to her sweaty forehead. "This will hurt, but you'll get used to it."

I position myself between her legs, my cockhead brushing her tight entrance. She bites her lip, breaths quick and shallow.

"Tonight changes everything," I growl, "You should've been a virgin on our wedding day but now you'll be pregnant with my baby when you walk down the aisle. I promise you that, darling."

I thrust into her, hard and brutal, tearing through the barrier of her virginity. She screams, hands flying to my shoulders, nails digging into my skin as I bury myself deep inside her. Pain crosses her features, tears filling her eyes, but she doesn't move, doesn't push away.

Her hot cunt grips my cock like a vise, drawing a groan

from me. I feel the warmth of her virgin blood trickling onto my cock, coating it, marking me. My lips draw back in a snarl as I pull back and thrust back in, harder.

"Be my good girl. Take the punishment you deserve for lying to me," I repeat, pumping in and out, each thrust deeper, more powerful than the last. Her fingernails leave deep half-moon cuts in my flesh, and the pain makes me grin. I love my little dove's fight. "Feel me fucking your pussy raw, marking you with my cock."

Her moans grow louder, deeper, mixed with whimpers of pain.

"Take me deeper," I growl, snapping my hips forward, filling her completely. "Your tight little pussy is perfect for my cock."

I grip her hips, pulling her into every thrust, watching her breasts bounce.

She moans louder, fingers raking across my back, leaving scratches, fresh wounds that sting and burn, that spur me on. I want her to feel every inch of my possession, every scream, every scar. I want her to understand what it means to belong to me, to sleep in my bed every night.

I grasp her neck, letting her feel the strength of my hands. She whimpers as the power within the hold I have on her reminds her of her place. I begin to fuck her in earnest, as soon as she capitulates, her hands go to the headboard, and she's desperate to hold on.

Her body tightens around me, begging for more. Her orgasm. She lets out a gasp, and her eyes widen as she feels the fullness of me stretching her.

Her eyes fill with tears.

I feel my climax building, the pressure in my balls ready to explode. I thrust deeper, harder, hitting her cervix with each stroke. She's so tight, so perfect. I can feel her body tensing, ready to come again. I reach between our bodies, finding her clit, and rub it.

I pinch her nipples, with my lips next to her own face. "Does that hurt, Zorina?'

She nods but strokes my back with delicate fingers.

"Come for me so I can breed your fertile cunt," I tell her.

She makes a tight noise.

The pleasure is excruciating, and I feel my release boiling close, my balls tightening, ready to erupt. "Where do you want my cum, baby? Tell me."

"Inside," she whimpers. "I want it inside me. Fill me up."

"Good girl," I praise, my cock slamming into her slick, heated channel. "I'm going to fill this pussy full until it's dripping out of you, till you feel my cum coating every part of you."

My thrusts grow frenzied, rough, and she meets them now, lifting her hips to take me deeper, willing and ready. I can feel the moment her orgasm hits, her body contracting around me, squeezing and milking every drop. I bellow, my own release exploding.

Everything I've been holding back rushes forth at once. A searing trail of pleasure climbs up my spine, melting my brain. Erasing every thought. Reducing the whole world to the heat of my seed pumping into her warm, unprotected pussy.

My seed spills into her endlessly, filling her to brimming, each thrust clicking me deeper inside her virgin cunt. Blinding pleasure slices me open. Her cunt is so tight, it heightens my orgasm even as I'm already emptying my balls inside her channel.

I stay in her longer, keeping her plugged up as I pinch her nipples, reminding her that I control her pleasure and her pain.

I collapse on top of her, our bodies slick with sweat, breaths mingling, hearts pounding in sync.

She's mine now, marked, owned, bred.

EIGHT

Zorina

THE ACHE between my thighs is unbearable.

Not sharp, not violent—just this low, molten throb that reminds me of everything Misha did to me last night. Every time I cross my legs on the padded bench, my muscles tighten around the ghost of his touch. My body still clenches like it's waiting for him to fill me again, and I hate how much I want it.

My nipples go stiff every time I relive the experience of Misha's hot, wet mouth molding to my hard nipples. He squeezed my tits roughly, desiring me, giving me everything.

I don't want to admit it but the sex was way better than I imagined it would be. It wasn't cold or efficient. It was white-hot, passionate, and all-consuming.

Mikhail made me come twice, and it was on the same night he took my virginity. My mother had always told me that I'd be aching and crying in pain when the time came to lose my virginity. While his cock's rough shocked me at first, the discomfort was over quickly. And then, he made me yearn for his deep, dominant strokes.

I submitted so naturally, my inner fire replaced by the feminine urge to be his vessel, to let his virile masculine ruin my womanhood. He possessed me completely, and I loved every moment of being filled by his thick cock, being pounded into like a breeding mare. His degradation and domination stimulated my psyche, my nerves, my brain. I wanted everything his dark whispers promised, and he delivered on all his claims.

Mikhail's skills in the bedroom are insane. I would never have known if he hadn't taken me.

The rehearsal room is drenched in pale morning light. Sunlight filters through the frosted glass panels, dust motes floating like lazy sparks. The Steinway grand in the center gleams under the light, its lid raised, its strings resonating faintly from the scales I've been forcing my fingers to run through. The air smells of polish and old wood. My violin case rests on the chair beside me, the velvet lining spilling a shadow across the floor.

I try to focus—Bach requires precision, not distraction. But my bow keeps trembling, slipping ever so slightly against the strings. The sound falters, as if the music itself knows my body isn't steady today.

The pianist, Marina, pauses mid-phrase. She's a slender woman in her forties with dark hair pinned in a low chignon, glasses perched on her nose. Patient, kind. She studies me the way a mother might study a restless child.

"You're tense," she observes, her accent lilting. "Something wrong?"

Before I can answer, the door creaks open. One of the stagehands slips inside, carrying a tray. On it—a tall cup of matcha latte, the foam decorated with an almost perfect swirl of cream, and a small packet of painkillers.

"From your fiancé," he says with a knowing smirk. "He said you'll need it."

My breath catches.

Misha.

I take the cup, the warmth seeping into my palms. My favorite drink. My exact brand. How did he even know? Then I remember he has his men trailing me at all times. Obviously, they keep notes about me. He must have gotten the information through them.

I glance at the painkillers, then at the man. "And Victor?" The words slip out before I can stop them.

The stagehand shrugs. "Don't know. Haven't seen him."

Which can only mean one thing—Misha had him removed. Quietly, efficiently. Like cutting out rot.

My chest tightens. I sip the matcha. Sweet, creamy, familiar. He did this for me. After everything that happened last night, after the way he claimed me in the dark like I belonged to him... he thought of me in the morning, too.

Marina smiles, nodding toward the tray. "Your fiancé is very sweet. Not many men think of small things like this. He's a rare one, Zorina. You're lucky."

Lucky.

The word echoes like a bow drawn too hard against a string.

Mikhail spoke of fate. That we were fated for each other. I know I can't avoid marrying him, and after last night, I don't want to. Whatever illusions I had about finding love with another man shattered the moment Victor grabbed my ass like I was a piece of meat. If Misha hadn't been there...I shudder to think what would have happened. Victor would have dragged me to the suite and done all kinds of terrible things to me. I doubt he'd have let me orgasm before he stuck his cock inside me.

I try to tell myself Misha did worse. He fucked me before our marriage, broke every vow and unspoken rule in the bratva.

But, technically, I was supposed to have married him five years ago.

Besides, seeing him snap, seeing him lose control and touch me made me realize that I'm not powerless. I used to think he didn't want me. That I couldn't do anything to make him touch me. But he desires me as fiercely as I desire him. He's powerless when he sees me in sexy outfits. If I want him to fuck me, all I have to do is show up at his house wearing a skimpy outfit.

But I won't. Because my pussy is still sore from losing my virginity. And Mikhail hasn't talked to me since he fucked me. Sure, he gave me aftercare, ordered room service, cleaned me with a wet towel, tucked me in, and let me stay at the suite all night.

But he never spoke a word. He never asked me how I was feeling. He definitely didn't tell me how he felt after taking my virginity. I know his armor cracked. He's just too proud to admit it.

But he can't avoid the truth forever. There's something between us. We're connected by years of acquaintance. There has always been something between us.

"Thinking of your fiancé?" Marina winks at me.

"Is it that obvious?"

I don't tell her what he did to me last night, how my knees nearly buckled as his mouth dragged every moan from my throat, how he made me feel both ruined and remade under his touch. But I can't ignore the truth: he wanted me to fall apart in his arms, and he didn't stop until I did. He put my pleasure first, even when he kept the rest of himself locked away.

And now all I can think about is the way his hands felt. The way I need them again.

I rub my sore thighs, hopeless against the ache. I can still feel the trickle of his cum as it slid down my thighs from my freshly-fucked cunt. How he dragged his fingers over my cum-slicked thighs and whispered, "You're mine for eternity, Zorina Antonova."

The matcha goes bitter on my tongue.

Tonight, I'll have to sit across from him at Leo Antonov's family dinner. All his brothers will be there—Leo with his assessing eyes, Aleksei with his brute force, and Dmitry with his quiet calculations. The thought of all of them in one room makes my stomach twist.

Misha will be beside me. Everyone will see.

I'll have to act like I'm calm. Like we didn't make love last night. Like he didn't fuck me into oblivion and call me by his last name.

THE ANTONOV MANSION rises from the Nevada desert like something out of a forgotten storybook. It has iron gates, marble columns, and chandeliers glittering like falling stars. I've been here many times, but nights like this always make me feel like I'm stepping into a lion's den.

I smooth the fabric of my dress before stepping into the grand dining hall. The gown is a little more daring than I usually wear—silk in a deep emerald shade that clings to my waist, the neckline cut just low enough to hint without revealing, the back a sloping plunge. I never thought of myself as bold when it came to clothes, but tonight... I wanted to be noticed.

"Beautiful," Leo says, rising from his chair at the head of the table. His gaze sweeps over me, assessing, appreciative but not lecherous. "That color suits you. Our mother would have said the same."

Heat flushes my cheeks. Before I can reply, I catch Mikhail's expression. His jaw is tight, lips pressed in a thin line. He looks like someone just put a gun to his temple. Angry. I wonder if he's still stinging from my betrayal with Victor. He hasn't said a word about it. Not to me, not to anyone. But silence can be worse than fury.

"Come," Leo murmurs, offering his arm. I take it, and he guides me to the table.

The table itself is a spectacle. Crystal candlesticks with flames that dance high, a buffet that could feed half of Moscow. Platters of pelmeni steaming in butter, bowls of bright-red borscht with sour cream swirling on top, golden piroshki stacked like treasure. Roasted duck glistening with glaze, black bread, smoked fish, and towers of blini with caviar. The scent of dill and garlic and roasted meat fills the hall until my stomach clenches in protest.

All the brothers are here, except Nikolai. That almost never happens. Leo is usually buried in Moscow, Aleksei prefers the city with his wife and daughter, Dmitry only visits when he can spare time from his endless spreadsheets at college. Family dinners like this—everyone under the same roof—happen maybe twice a year. And thank God for that.

Misha lives here, either with Nikolai or alone, depending on the season. Tonight, I'll be sitting beside him in front of all his brothers.

Dmitry looks up from his seat with a rare smile. His face is sharper than his brothers', his eyes like cut glass behind that reserved demeanor. "Zorina," he says warmly, surprising me. "Glad you could join us."

Beside him, Aleksei rises half out of his chair. He's massive, built like a wall, but when he greets me, I see the softness he's grown into since marriage. His smile is genuine, his shoulders less tense than I remember. He looks like a family man now, softened around the edges by love, though I know he can still snap a man's spine without blinking.

"Where's Nikolai?" I ask as I take my seat. The youngest Antonov always brought a spark of mischief to the table.

"At school," Leo says smoothly, reaching for his wine. "A boarding school in England."

I blink. "England?"

Dmitry chuckles under his breath, leaning back in his chair. "He got expelled from the last one. Leo paid a fortune to secure him a place at an elite school. Somewhere he can learn restraint—and hopefully graduate without burning the place down."

A pang of longing twists through me. I miss him. Nikolai was fun, reckless, irreverent. He made the mansion feel less like a fortress.

I turn to Aleksei. "And your daughter? How is she?"

The man beams. The brute melts right in front of me, eyes glowing with pride. "Perfect. She and Lena are at home tonight. Lena's expecting again." His voice softens, almost reverent. "I can't wait to go back to them."

The pang sharpens. His wife has everything I want—her husband's love, his devotion, their children. And theirs wasn't an arrangement born out by blood and politics. Lena is much younger than Aleksei. She attended the same university as Dmitry. They fell in love while doing dangerous missions together as part of the secret society the Antonov brothers control at Allister College.

It's an action-packed love story. I'd love to hear all the details from Lena one day, but she doesn't come to these family dinners. I guess it's because she's heavily pregnant and she can't strain herself. Aleksei is very protective of her. Besides, it's an open secret that Leo doesn't particularly like her because she's American, not Russian like me. He even endangered her life in Moscow once. I don't think Aleksei has forgiven him for that yet.

I glance at Mikhail beside me. He pours wine into my glass without looking at me, his face carved from ice. Colder than he was before. Is it still about Victor? Is that why he won't meet my eyes? Or is it because I let him fuck me even though I'm supposed to be a virgin on our wedding night? It's hard to read him, and he doesn't communicate.

I reach under the table, brushing my fingers against his hand. For a second, he lets me. Then he withdraws, lifting his fork instead. The rejection stings. I don't know where we stand anymore.

Leo clears his throat, voice commanding. "Soon, you and Mikhail will be husband and wife. Less than a year now. I've booked a fitting for you in Moscow—one of the best boutiques. The same atelier that made Lena's gown. And our mother's, too."

My chest lifts with excitement despite myself. Moscow. It's been years.

The brothers join in, their banter warm and teasing. Aleksei tells me to make sure Mikhail doesn't cut corners on the flowers. Dmitry smirks, suggesting he can negotiate discounts with vendors if I ask him nicely.

I laugh softly, admitting, "I've been so focused on my last album, on rehearsals... I haven't thought about wedding details."

"She doesn't need to," Mikhail says at last, his voice low and even. "We'll hire planners. She doesn't need to worry about the minutiae."

Dmitry smirks. "Protecting your investment, brother? Making sure her album pays out before she's too distracted by bridal fittings?"

Laughter ripples around the table, but my heart beats differently. Because I know it's not just about investment.

Mikhail doesn't want me to get overwhelmed by wedding planning. Once, before, when I was much younger, I told him I didn't want to spend a year of my life just thinking of cake flavors and party decorations. That I didn't want my mind to be taken up by such trivial things because I wanted to focus on playing the violin and improving my craft. Perhaps, he assumes that's still the case.

I don't correct him. I'm definitely not looking forward to table arrangements. I know I'll have to host parties for his business associates once we're married, but this is the last year of freedom I have. The last chance I have to become his lover, the woman he needs and loves, not a pretty hostess in his home.

The laughter around the table echoes in my chest. The brothers are chatty and rambunctious as usual. I don't have to fill in any awkward silences, or smooth over any arguments. I can just eat.

I've been part of this family so long that their comfort with me feels real. It makes me ache. Because sometimes, I forget the line between belonging and being owned.

The wine is warm against my tongue, but the warmth does nothing to ease the tension knotted in my shoulders. The brothers are in good spirits, and when they are together like this, I'm always their favorite target.

"So," Aleksei says, pointing a fork at me, his grin mischievous, "have you tamed him yet, Zorina?"

I blink. "Tamed?"

"Yes," Dmitry murmurs, adjusting his glass with precise fingers. "Misha. He doesn't exactly... bend easily. Or at all. And he never says sentimental things like 'I love you'." His mouth curves in the faintest of smiles. "I'd be impressed if you've managed it."

Heat prickles my neck. "I... wouldn't say that."

"She has him wrapped around her little finger," Aleksei declares, winking at me. "Don't be fooled by his scowl. A woman who can get Mikhail Antonov to bring her tea and painkillers is already winning."

My chest stutters. They know. Somehow they know about the matcha latte, about the gesture that made my heart trip this morning.

"Don't tease her," Leo says mildly, though his eyes glint. "Zorina's been patient. More patient than most women would be."

"That's one word for it," Dmitry mutters.

Laughter ripples around the table, all except Mikhail. His hand stills on the stem of his glass, and I can feel the storm building in him.

"She doesn't need to tame me," Mikhail says suddenly, his voice low, cutting across the table. "I am already hers."

The room goes silent. My pulse spikes. He said it like it was a matter-of-fact. I know Mikhail has never cheated on me. He's been faithful, even though we're not even married yet. Men are allowed to do whatever they want in the bratva. He could have fifteen mistresses in four continents and I couldn't do anything about it. But he respects the institution of marriage. And, in a way, I guess he respects me. He doesn't want me to compete for attention. All of his attention is mine, even if I never know what to do with it.

Aleksei's brows lift, his grin widening. "Possessive, are we?"

Mikhail's gaze doesn't leave me. His expression is carved from stone, but his words slice through every nerve in my body. "She's mine. That's all anyone here needs to know."

My lips part, useless, as the brothers burst into laughter again—half mocking, half surprised, all too entertained by the rare show of temper from their most controlled brother.

I can hardly taste the food anymore. My body hums with equal parts fear and exhilaration. He's staking a claim in front of them, a claim no one can mistake.

And for the first time tonight, I wonder if beneath that cold façade, the man beside me is as close to shattering as I am.

I reach for the platter of roasted duck at the same time Mikhail does. My fingers graze his knuckles, and he jerks his hand back like I've burned him.

The movement is so sharp, so deliberate, that the entire table goes silent for a beat.

Then Dmitry chuckles low, a blade hidden in velvet. "Careful, Zorina. If you keep startling him like that, he might never eat again."

Aleksei leans back, grinning, arms crossed over his chest. "If he keeps pulling away like that, she'll still be untouched when they're married." His voice carries amusement, but his eyes are keen, watching for a reaction.

Blood rushes to my cheeks. They don't know. They can't know. But Mikhail's reaction makes them suspicious, and their laughter only grows.

Inside, I know the truth—he's not recoiling because he doesn't want me. He's recoiling because he touched me last night. Because he broke his own rules, and now he doesn't know how to act when we're surrounded by witnesses.

Leo lifts a hand, silencing the noise. His expression is unreadable, but there's a spark of something calculating in his eyes. "Enough," he says, voice smooth as steel. "I think the solution is simple. We give them a trial run. A honeymoon test."

My fork clatters against the plate. "A... what?"

"A trip," Leo clarifies. "In two weeks, Mikhail is flying to Miami on business. She'll go with him. She can work on her album tracks at the hotel while he attends meetings. They'll have time together. Get used to each other before the wedding."

My stomach twists. Miami. Alone with him, when I can hardly breathe sitting beside him now. "Leo, I—"

"It's perfect," Aleksei cuts in, smirking. "A little sun, a little sea, a little romantic bonding."

"I don't think—" My voice cracks, too weak against theirs.

"Her father will never allow it." Mikhail's voice cuts through, sharp. He sets his glass down, the stem ringing against the crystal. "Vadim is a conservative man. Spending nights together before marriage is unthinkable."

"You don't need to share a room," Leo says smoothly, unbothered. "Vadim will understand. He knows you need time together before the wedding. He'll want this union to be strong."

Mikhail's jaw tightens. "It's unsafe. Miami isn't our territory."

Aleksei laughs, leaning forward. "You're the one handling security, brother. If it's unsafe, that's your failure."

Dmitry adds dryly, "Unless you're really just worried you can't handle being in the same city as her without combusting."

Heat curls low in my stomach. They're pushing him, stripping away his excuses one by one. I can feel Mikhail's fury, the weight of it pressing off him in waves.

"We don't have the time," he tries again, voice gritted.

"Make time," Leo answers, his final word carrying the weight of command. "It's decided. Miami."

Mikhail's chest swells on a forced inhale. Tension wraps around his eyes, deepening is crow's feet and the lines on his forehead. Leo has made the decision. He's the pakhan. Mikhail doesn't have the authority to refuse. His helplessness is written all over the way he grabs his glass of wine and chugs it down.

The brothers toast the decision with a chorus of raised

glasses, laughter echoing under the chandelier. Celebration, victory, amusement at watching their icy brother cornered.

I sit frozen, the stem of my wineglass slippery between my fingers. My pulse beats fast. I lean closer, lowering my voice so only Mikhail hears me. "Is this... is this okay?"

For a moment, he doesn't move. Then, under the table, his hand closes hard around my thigh, hot through the silk of my dress. He squeezes, firm enough to steal my breath.

He tilts his head, finally meeting my eyes. His mouth barely moves, his words a lethal whisper.

"In Miami, you'll learn exactly what it means to be mine."

The world tilts, the laughter of his brothers fading into static. My chest tightens with fear, with heat, with a hunger I can't name.

And I know—I'm trapped. With a man who could destroy me.

NINE

Mikhail

THE LOUNGE IS DIM, private, cocooned in velvet and smoke. Gold sconces cast soft light over the mahogany-paneled walls, and the faint scent of expensive cigars lingers despite the no-smoking rule. Only we are allowed to break the rules here.

A round table of black marble sits in the center, already scattered with bottles of Beluga vodka, tumblers of whiskey, and cut crystal shot glasses. It's not a ritual, but the kind of thing we do occasionally, when we're in the mood and all in the same city—no outsiders, no women, just the Antonov brothers unwinding in the belly of one of our casinos.

Leo sits at the head, as always, his suit impeccable, his expression already tight with the beginnings of a headache. Aleksei sprawls in his chair, massive and relaxed, the scar along his jaw catching the light when he grins. Dmitry looks bored, as if his laptop should be on the table instead of a glass.

I pour myself a shot of vodka, the burn sharp against my throat.

Leo sighs, rubbing his temple. "I called Nikolai's school today. Guess who answered?"

Aleksei laughs. "Don't tell me it was a headmaster."

"A prefect," Leo mutters darkly. "A girl. Said she confiscated his phone because he was texting in class."

I smirk into my glass. "Already?"

"Already," Leo snaps. "Two weeks in and he's causing trouble. He was supposed to learn restraint."

Dmitry snorts. "Restraint? That word isn't in his vocabulary."

"He's an Antonov," Aleksei says with a shrug. "What did you expect? At least he's consistent."

The room fills with laughter, the easy banter that comes when we remember we're not just Bratva, but brothers. But it never stays light for long. Not with us.

Leo's gaze shifts to me, sharp and deliberate. "Speaking of restraint. You need to make more effort with Zorina."

The laughter dies. My jaw tightens. "My marriage is not open for commentary."

Leo leans forward, his voice low, even. "If she runs before the wedding, Vadim will never forgive us. That alliance will crumble, and you know what that means."

"She won't run." I take another shot, cold settling in my chest. "She can do what she wants—shop, travel, play her music. I keep her satisfied. I don't oppress her like her father does."

Leo doesn't flinch. "She looks scared, Misha. And she shouldn't fear her husband. We're Bratva, yes. But we're still family men."

Family men. I almost laugh. That word doesn't belong to me.

Besides, the reason Zorina is scared is because I let my control shatter. I let my baser instincts get the better of me. I pushed her fertile, untouched body against a wall and kissed her. I pressed her body down on the bed and fucked her until she cried my name. And she was not ready. It was too soon. She bled and she whimpered. She came on my cock and my tongue. But she wasn't ready to be fucked like that. It shocked her.

I resisted touching her for years because of her age, but even now, she's still young. I should have known that.

She seems more guarded since that night. Distant. She talks to me like she's not sure what I'll do next. I need to talk to her. But I don't know what to say. I'm too possessive to apologize. I try to show her my gratitude in small ways. I sent her an Hermes handbag two days after our night at the hotel. I didn't want her to feel forgotten after we're been intimate. I send her small things—bracelets, hot compresses, tea—because that's the only way I know how to show affection, even though I know she craves heartfelt conversations and physical intimacy.

Where she's concerned, there's no chance of slow, easy lovemaking. She makes my cock explode with heat. I can't do slow and sensual when all I want is to be buried inside her.

Victor is out of her life for good now, so at least I don't have to worry about him anymore.

"She's not shallow," Leo presses, softer now. "She defied her father for her music, for her freedom. She's passionate. That's exactly what you've locked away inside yourself."

The silence thickens. I look away, swirling the vodka in my glass.

In my mind, I'm back in that hotel room. Her lips bruised, her voice hoarse from begging, her body trembling as I gave her what she didn't even know she craved. Raw. Uncontrolled. Reckless.

I press the memory down, hard.

Am I passionate? Was that passion? Or was it just animalistic lust, an instinct to possess something I instinctively sense belongs to me?

There are no happy endings. I've seen what happens when men give in to that illusion—it ends in betrayal, in blood.

But Zorina's fire... it might be dangerous enough to melt through walls I've kept fortified my entire life.

I drain the glass, vowing silently, fiercely: No more mistakes. No more recklessness. In Miami, I'll keep my hands off her. No distractions. No weakness.

And definitely no pregnancy before the wedding, even if the thought of Zorina's belly swollen under her wedding dress makes me hard.

I pour another shot, the vodka sharp on my tongue. Silence doesn't last long with this family. It never does.

"You say she can do whatever she wants," Dmitry says, his tone as dry as the desert outside. He twirls the glass in his hand, unimpressed. "But you sound more like an accountant balancing a ledger than a fiancé. Does she even know you can be human?"

My eyes cut to him, cold. "Careful, brat."

He lifts a shoulder, unfazed. "Just asking."

Aleksei leans forward, resting his massive arms on the table, grin wide and taunting. "He's right, though. You treat her like a child you've been saddled with. She's a fully-grown woman with talents, opinions, and experiences. Have you ever tried knowing more about her?"

"I don't treat her like a child," I bite out, harsher than intended, my mind tripping back to the night when I tasted her pussy. I was definitely treating her like a woman.

Aleksei whistles low. "Finally, some fire. Haven't heard that tone from you in a long time. Maybe she does get under your skin."

"She doesn't," I say, but the lie tastes bitter.

Leo steeples his fingers, watching me the way a general watches a soldier about to break formation. "Zorina isn't afraid of passion, Misha. She's afraid of indifference. Maybe that's why she fears you."

Does she fear me? Is that why she seeks to escape with men like Victor, men who open up easily and can make declarations of love at the drop of a hat?

"You're afraid of your own feelings for her," Aleksei says, clapping his hand on my back. "You say you don't feel anything for her, but you take care of her. You keep a watch on her and protect her. You wouldn't do that unless she meant something. Maybe it's time to stop lying to yourself and embrace the fact that she interests you in ways you don't like being interested."

I set my glass down hard enough to crack the silence. "Enough. When did our poker night turn into a self-development lecture?"

Dmitry scoffs. "He's just grumpy because he's losing."

Aleksei chuckles. "You're so wound up you might snap before the wedding. Maybe that's why Leo suggested the honeymoon trial."

Nobody can make my brothers shut up when they've decided to gang up on me. Leo is usually quiet, but I know he's interested in my marriage because it's tied to the future of our organization.

Leo's voice is calm, final. "You'll take her to Miami. And you'll show her something other than cold silence. Something that will make her stay."

I glare at him. "You presume too much."

"No," Leo says, his gaze locking mine. "I lead this family. And I know the cost of letting alliances fracture. You'll woo her in Miami, Mikhail. Whether you like it or not. Give her the nice words she needs. Who knows? It might be therapeutic to let out everything than you've been holding back for years. You have a lot to talk about, don't you?"

The words land heavy, unshakable.

I drink again, the vodka a poor substitute for control. My brothers are laughing now, jabbing at each other, at me, celebrating the small victory of watching me cornered. They don't see the way my hands tighten, the way my blood runs hotter with every mocking word.

But inside, I'm already making another vow.

If Zorina comes to Miami, she'll see a side of me I've buried for years.

And I don't know if that will keep her... or break her.

TEN

Zorina

THE CASES LINE the bed like silent witnesses—Louis Vuitton leather in soft cream, already stuffed with silk blouses, sundresses, delicate lingerie I folded with shaking hands. Miami. The word makes my pulse quicken.

I tuck another dress inside, the fabric slipping through my fingers like water, when my mother appears in the doorway. She glides across the room, perfume heavy and sharp, eyes scanning my choices with thinly veiled disdain.

"Too plain," she mutters, lifting one of my dresses with two manicured fingers. "You'll bore him. Men stray, Zorina. Remember that."

The words cut sharper than she intends. My father strayed more times than I can count, his affairs paraded in whispers that circled our home like ghosts. But I keep my mouth shut. Confronting her won't change the truth.

When I wheel the cases downstairs, my father waits at

the bottom of the staircase. His gaze is hard, unrelenting. "Behave yourself," he says, his voice like a gavel. "Don't give him any reason to doubt you. A proper lady doesn't tempt scandal."

The reprimand lingers, heavy and unfair, but I bite my tongue. Silence is easier than war.

Outside, Misha's chauffeur stands by the black Maybach, the door open in silent invitation. My father's lips curl into a cold smile as I pass him. "Finally learning your place."

The words ignite something rebellious in me, small but dangerous. I keep walking, refusing to look back.

The car smells faintly of leather and cedarwood when I step inside. And there he is—Mikhail in a charcoal suit, white shirt open at the collar, his tie discarded. His cologne wraps around me, dark and intoxicating. One breath of it and my knees threaten to give way. I want to straddle him right here, in front of his driver, bury my face in his throat.

But I sit primly beside him instead, clutching my hands in my lap.

"We just need to get this over with," he says without looking at me, his tone clipped.

I nod, the words catching in my throat. Then, to my shock, he reaches down and produces a bouquet of pale pink roses.

My heart stutters. "What... are you doing?"

His lips twitch in something almost like mockery. "Wooing you."

The air rushes out of me. "You're—wooing me?"

"Yes." His tone is flat, almost clinical. "Leo asked me to make the effort. You may report back to him that I complied."

The fragile bloom of hope inside me withers instantly. I press the flowers to my lap, their softness mocking me.

The Maybach eases away from the curb. Misha leans back, his profile cut in shadow, jaw tight enough to crack. He doesn't speak for several minutes, and when he does, his voice is pure steel.

"The itinerary is tight. Meetings in the morning, dinners with partners in the evenings. I'll need you presentable for one gala, nothing more. The rest of the time, you'll stay out of sight."

I glance out the tinted window, my chest aching. "Miami has beaches," I say softly. "We could—"

He cuts me off, his voice sharp. "We're going there for work, not pleasure."

The flowers in my lap feel heavy, pointless.

"You'll stay in your own room," he continues, his tone leaving no room for negotiation. "Use the hotel's spa, the pool. Think about your next album. Relax. You've been working hard. Consider it a break."

I stare down at the roses, their petals trembling with the car's movement. For a moment, I almost believe him. That this is about rest. That this is care. But then I catch the way his jaw clenches again, the way he avoids looking at me.

And I know the truth: he's putting walls back up. Walls I'm not sure I'll ever be able to climb.

The roses tremble in my lap with every turn of the car. Their sweetness fills the confined space, but it feels cloying, suffocating. Finally, I press them back into his hands.

"I don't need these," I whisper. My throat feels tight. "I'll tell Leo whatever he wants to hear. But don't deceive me unless you really plan to woo me."

His brows lift, a flicker of something passing through his expression. For a moment I expect the cutting line—why would he woo me when I already belong to him? But it doesn't come.

Instead, his jaw slackens. He looks at me—really looks—and something gentles in his eyes. "I'm... sorry," he says at last, the words low, rough.

I suck in a shocked breath. "You... apologized."

He nods once, a brief dip of his chin. "I didn't mean to confuse you."

My voice shakes. "It wasn't the flowers that confused me, Misha. It was the false hope."

His gaze darkens. He turns the roses over in his hand, the petals brushing his knuckles. "I didn't mean the flowers," he murmurs. His voice is lower now, intimate, dangerous. "I meant the night at the hotel."

Heat floods my chest. The memory slams into me—the press of his mouth, the rough grip of his hands, the way he shattered every boundary in a single night.

"It was..." His jaw tightens. "A momentary insanity. I couldn't control myself when I saw you looking like that. So sexy it drove me mad."

I shift, breath unsteady. "Would you do it again?"

His eyes lock with mine, burning. "Yes." The word is raw, torn from somewhere deep. "Because it's no lie when I say I find you physically attractive. Your body. Your spirit. The fire you carry—it ignites something base in me."

I can't move. Can't breathe.

He gestures at me, his gaze flicking over my outfit—my high-neck blouse, my tailored pants. "That's why you must dress like this. Demure. Modest. And you must stay out of my sight. Unless you want a repeat of that night."

My thighs press together involuntarily, desperate for relief. My skin burns where it brushes his, a fleeting contact when the car jolts. Sparks shoot up my leg.

His breath catches, and then—he shifts sharply, putting inches between us. "Your warmth, your softness—it's addictive," he mutters, almost to himself. "But I won't let it cloud my judgment again. Not unless..." His mouth curves in a wicked smile. "Not unless you plan to cheat on me again. Then, all bets are off."

His teasing shouldn't send shivers down my spine, but it does.

"You think you hurt me that night," I say softly, summoning courage from somewhere fragile. "But you didn't. I liked it."

The car stills. His hand tightens around the bouquet until a petal tears free, fluttering to the floor. His eyes soften, the sharp lines of his face easing into something that makes my chest ache.

"You liked it," he repeats, voice low, roughened.

"Yes." I draw a breath, heart hammering. "I didn't expect it to. But I did. It felt... good."

For the first time in years, tenderness flickers across his face. His fingers brush mine—light, tentative, but enough to send lightning racing through me.

And I know—I've finally cracked his pride.

THE ANTONOV JET is a palace in the sky—cream leather seats, polished wood paneling, golden sconces that cast a soft glow. A Persian rug runs the aisle, muffling the hum of engines, while discreet attendants move with the quiet elegance of ghosts. A tray of champagne flutes glimmers under the light, paired with tiny towers of caviar on blini, smoked salmon pinwheels, and glossy macarons arranged like jewels.

I sip the champagne slowly, the bubbles sharp and ticklish on my tongue. The taste is decadent, like secrets kept too long. I've never flown like this before. For me, travel meant cramped tour buses and long waits at airport security. This—this is something I used to dream about.

"You look happy," Misha says, his voice low, cutting into my thoughts.

I glance at him. He lounges across from me, long legs stretched out, his tie loosened at the throat. The sight makes him look... softer somehow. Almost human.

"I like fine things," I admit with a small smile. "I've never been on a private jet before."

He makes a noncommittal sound, as if the champagne and the Persian rugs and the luxury mean nothing. And maybe they don't. He's lived with this his whole life. For me, it's new. For me, it still dazzles.

He pulls out his wallet to make a call. Something slips free, fluttering down like a secret escaping.

A photograph.

I reach for it before I can think, fingers brushing against the rug. A young man stares up at me from the glossy print. Strong jaw, laughing eyes, caught in a candid moment.

"Who's this?" I ask softly.

The effect is immediate. Misha goes still. His entire body stiffens, muscles tightening beneath his suit. He leans forward, snatching the photograph from my hand. For a second, I think he might snap at me. But when he looks up, his eyes are clouded—not with rage, but sorrow.

Long silence stretches between us. Finally, he exhales, the sound heavy. "A brother who's no longer with us. Someone who was more loyal than blood."

My chest aches. "What happened?"

"Rolan." His voice roughens on the name. "My cousin. Shot. Because he trusted the wrong people."

I set my champagne aside, leaning in, urging him gently.

"We walked into an ambush. He died protecting me." Each word is clipped, precise, like he's forcing them out.

I swallow hard, watching the pain flicker across his features.

"He trusted a woman," Misha adds, his voice sharpening. "Loved her. They were going to get married. He thought he'd found his soulmate. But she sold him out. She was working with my closest ally. The two of them laughing at his sentimentality while they put a bullet through his chest."

My breath catches. His hand curls into a fist, and my gaze drifts to the faint, jagged scar across his palm.

Suddenly, it all makes sense. His emotional guardedness. His lack of desire to fall in love. To him, love is betrayal. Death. Foolishness. That's all he has seen. He doesn't know that love is freedom, joy, and trust, too.

"You survived," I whisper, as if trying to tell him that love won't kill him.

He follows my eyes. Slowly, deliberately, he opens his hand, scarred lines pale against his skin. "The ambush. When I realized he'd been betrayed. I barely walked away alive."

His gaze snaps to mine, sharp as glass, glittering with warning and something else—something raw, unguarded.

"I don't take betrayal lightly anymore," he says, gravel in his tone. "I punish it. Ruthlessly. Lies get people killed in my world."

A shiver runs down my spine. Now I finally know the depth of the scars he has been carrying, the reason he runs from the thought of intimacy. He is scared of trusting me. Of trusting himself to make the right judgment where a woman is concerned. Maybe that's why he let Leo arrange his marriage instead of choosing a partner himself. He trusts Leo to pick wisely. His other brothers all scoff at the idea of an arranged marriage, preferring to pick their partners themselves. Even Leo himself has never married, no matter how tempting the alliance may be.

They all have faith in their own choices. But Mikhail doesn't. I'm safe, because I was picked by Leo. But seeing me with Victor at the hotel must have made him question everything.

I wet my lips, daring to ask, "Is that why you don't believe in love?"

The silence that follows is louder than the engines. His gaze doesn't waver, but he doesn't speak. And in that wordless void, I already know the answer.

ELEVEN

Mikhail

THE ENGINES' roar has faded, replaced by the hushed shuffle of attendants preparing the jet for landing. Miami sprawls beneath us, glittering with neon and saltwater haze, the ocean catching the last of the sun like fire.

But all I can feel is the hollow weight in my chest.

I've never spoken about Rolan to anyone outside my brothers. Never. That scar on my palm has been my private brand, a reminder of what trust costs, of how love destroys. But tonight, on that damn jet, she looked at me with those wide, earnest eyes and I—God help me—I let it slip. Words I swore would stay buried spilled into the air between us.

And when she listened... when she didn't flinch or judge... something loosened inside me. The burden I've carried alone for years shifted, just enough for me to feel it.

Now it terrifies me.

Because she knows. She knows the story, the scar, the way

I've bled. She knows too much. And knowledge is power, one I've been betrayed with before.

I glance at her as the jet descends. She sits by the window, lips parted, gaze drinking in the skyline as if it's the first sunrise she's ever seen. Innocent. Beautiful. Dangerous.

The car waiting for us is sleek and black, whisking us into the heart of the city. Palms blur past, lights flickering, heat already pressing in. By the time we arrive at the hotel, my jaw aches from being clenched so long.

The lobby is marble and glass, a chandelier dripping with crystals overhead. Attendants rush forward, bowing, offering champagne, speaking in the reverent hush reserved for billionaires. Zorina looks around with awe, her smile tugging at something buried in me.

At the reception desk, the concierge hands me two key cards. I catch her hesitation when she realizes what it means.

"Separate rooms," I say, my tone brisk. "It's better this way."

Her smile falters, but she nods, slipping her key into her clutch. We ride the elevator in silence, our reflections ghosting across polished metal. When the doors open, her suite is just across from mine—too close, too tempting.

I open her door for her, letting her step inside first. The suite is drenched in gold and cream, floor-to-ceiling windows spilling moonlight across the king-sized bed. For a second, I imagine her tangled in those sheets, my hands on her thighs, her moans muffled by the night sky. Heat surges through me, violent, unwanted.

I force myself to turn away. Restraint. I need restraint.

Still, I linger in the doorway, watching her set down her bag, watching the way her dress shifts against her body. Something inside me cracks. I step forward, my hand brushing hers before I can stop myself.

"Thank you," I murmur, my voice rough.

She looks up, startled. "For what?"

"For listening to me. On the plane." My thumb skims over her knuckles before I pull back. "I don't... do that. Talk."

Her lips curve into the smallest smile. "I liked it. I liked that you talked to me."

The words sink into me deeper than I want them to. Maybe Leo was right. Maybe this—whatever this is—could be therapy. Wooing, he called it. God, the man will laugh if he ever hears me admit it.

I clear my throat, stepping back toward the hall before I forget myself. "Get dressed. I'll shower and come get you in a few minutes. We'll eat dinner together."

Her eyes widen, then brighten. The glow in her face is so pure it knocks the breath from me. She's... excited. Just because I offered to sit at a table with her.

And damn me, but seeing her happy makes me feel lighter. Joyful, even.

I leave her there with her joy, clutching the thin thread of control I have left.

THE RESTAURANT IS PERCHED HIGH above the city, windows stretched from floor to ceiling so the lights below glitter like scattered diamonds. The table is set with polished silver, linen napkins, and candles flickering low, throwing soft shadows against Zorina's skin.

And her dress.

My grip on the stem of my wineglass tightens. The fabric is silk, crimson, clinging to every curve. The neckline dips scandalously low, a whisper away from indecent, the straps so thin I could snap them with a finger. Her shoulders gleam under the candlelight, smooth and bare.

"Who told you to wear that?" The words are sharper than I intend.

She startles slightly, then lifts her chin. "My mother. She forced me to pack it. Said I need to seduce you before you start cheating on me."

I drag my gaze from her collarbone to her eyes, fury and desire twisting inside me like barbed wire. She shouldn't look like this. Not here. Not with other men watching.

But God, she's exquisite.

I take a slow sip of wine, forcing my hand to steady. Resist. I can't let her see how badly I want to reach across the table, pull her to me, mark her until no man dares look again.

Instead, I say, "I don't like it."

Her lips twitch, almost a smile. "That's the point, isn't it? To make you uncomfortable?"

The audacity. I almost laugh, but the sound catches in my throat.

We eat in silence for a while, the hum of conversation around us filling the gaps.

"Were you always like this?" Zorina's question shatters the peaceful quietness. "Even when you were young, were you always so emotionally reserved?"

Almost against my will, I speak.

"When I was a boy," I say, my voice low, "I idolized Leo. He was older, stronger. He was everything I wanted to be."

Zorina looks up, startled. I don't usually give pieces of myself away. Not like this.

"Our father..." I pause, the word sour in my mouth. "He was a hard man. Brutal. His approval came only through fear, through violence. I learned early that softness meant weakness. To survive, I had to fight and bleed."

The candlelight flickers against the rim of my glass. I stare into it, seeing the ghosts of our childhood home, the blood-soaked lessons I can never unlearn.

"Everything I own," I continue, the words bitter, "every ounce of respect I command—it's all drenched in blood. Nothing more."

Silence settles between us, heavier than the Miami heat pressing against the windows.

Then, softly, her hand stretches across the table. Tentative. Hesitant. She brushes her fingertips against mine, then slides to the jagged scar in my palm.

I don't pull away.

Her touch is light, reverent, like she's tracing a wound in stained glass. For a moment, I let her. For a moment, the walls I've built so carefully crack.

And in that fragile silence, something dangerous blooms.

The crimson silk of her dress catches every candle flame, turning her into a living spark. The neckline plunges indecently low, her bare shoulders glowing, her hair falling soft around her face. My gut twists with hunger and fury all at once.

I should tell her to change. I should drag her back upstairs and wrap her in something that hides her from the eyes roving across this room. But instead, I drink her in, silently cursing myself for being weak.

Her laughter, light and uncertain, breaks the silence between us. She reaches across the table, brushing her fingers over the scar in my palm again. I freeze, my body taut, but I don't pull away.

"What do you feel when you touch me like that?" I ask before I can stop myself.

Her cheeks flush pink. She looks down, voice barely audible. "Your heartbeat."

The answer coils around my chest, tightening. "Do you like feeling it?"

She nods, meeting my gaze. "For those few seconds, your heart is only mine. It belongs to me. At least... that's what I think." She gives a nervous laugh, eyes shimmering. "You must think I'm a hopeless romantic."

The expression on her face, sad, hopeful, fragile, cuts deeper than I expect. I realize, with a sick twist of guilt, how often I've hurt her without meaning to. How she longs for something I may never be able to give her. Love.

But I can give her what I do have. My loyalty. My body. My commitment.

"You're not wrong," I tell her, voice low. "My heart is yours. Even when you're not touching me. Along with the rest of me. My body. My name. They're yours. Just as you are mine."

The air thickens, the candle flames trembling as if they feel it too. Her breath hitches, her eyes wide, luminous.

I lean forward, slowly, deliberately, giving her a chance to retreat. She doesn't. Her lips part, a soft invitation, and I take it.

My palm is stretching across the back of her head before I can overthink my actions. My lips press against hers, brushing over the softness of her mouth. Her feminine lips mold to me like they're made of velvet. God, that would feel divine wrapped around my cock.

Unlike our previous kisses, tonight, I take my time savoring her sweetness. Our tongues mingle in a slow-burning reaction. I feel the fireworks exploding behind my eyes moments later, when she responds to me, brushing her tongue along the side of mine, giving me the friction I desperately crave.

My blood heats. The flow of blood intensifies. I can't hear anything except the rush in my head. The slow, all-consuming taste of her fills my mouth and blooms like a wound inside my body. She's making my system bleed, like she cut an organ inside my body, when all she did was press her mouth to mine. Yet, I feel naked. As if she turned me inside out. I've never felt so vulnerable while kissing anyone. It's like she plucked out all my secrets, and all I have left are the empty spaces where I used to hide the things I didn't want her to see.

Those spaces, dark and lonely, sting a little more every time she showers me with her pure, devoted love. Her tiny fingers catch on my shirt, seeking my strength, aching for my warmth.

It feels incredible to be needed and desired by her. Zorina has no agenda. Except to learn the taste of my mouth.

This kiss is slow, reverent, my mouth molding against hers with care. Her lips are warm, pliant, tasting faintly of champagne and strawberries.

I suck on her bottom lip. Her fullness satisfies me in a way I can't describe. My gut clenches when she moves her mouth against mine. I chase the electric burst that follows the heady brush of our lips, needing the high she gives me.

My fingers dig into her hair, dragging over her scalp.

She whimpers into my mouth like a needy, wounded animal. It feels like someone sliced my chest with a knife. The pain and shattered hopes she hides in her tiny moan pricks into me like shards of glass, lodging into my psyche, cutting me open. Demanding that I heal her, return the innocence she lost by loving me for years.

But I can't. I am afraid of giving her all of me. I protect my heart because the past has taught me that it's the only way to protect myself from betrayal.

All I can do is offer her a cheap, superficial version of romance and hope that she mistakes it for the real thing.

We both come up for air. That's when I know Zorina is not one to be deceived easily.

Her whole face is flushed scarlet, but her eyes aren't twinkling with the kind of joy lovers share. She blinks, dazed, then whispers, "Why... why did you do that?"

"Because I wanted to." My thumb brushes her cheek. "I don't hate that you're a hopeless romantic, Zorina. But I can never be one. And you may have a hard time accepting that."

She laughs softly, shaking her head. Her fingers lift again, finding the pulse at my wrist. "I think deep inside, you are one, too."

My brows knit. "Why?"

"Because when we kissed," she murmurs, "your pulse jumped. And if fate brought us together... fate wouldn't bother unless we were similar in some way. I believe all connections have meaning."

Her words linger, sinking into me. She looks so sure, so certain, while I'm drowning in the storm inside my head.

Care. That's what I felt when I saw the sadness on her face. The sudden, desperate urge to erase it. That isn't romance. It's instinct. Protection.

And yet... under the Miami sky, with her lips still warm on mine, it felt like something more.

Maybe I am losing my mind here, alone with her. Or maybe she's right. Maybe, buried beneath scars and blood, there's a romantic in me after all.

And Zorina Morozova might be the only woman in the world who can bring out that man.

TWELVE

Zorina

THE NIGHT FEELS DIFFERENT. Something has shifted between us—subtle, fragile, but real. For six years I've lived with his silence, his distance. Tonight, he's let me see behind the walls. Just a glimpse. Just enough to make me ache for more.

But I don't push. If I press too hard, he'll retreat. And I can't bear the thought of him shutting me out again.

We leave the restaurant, the warm Miami air wrapping around us. I expect him to march me back to my room, to slam the door on whatever connection we'd found over dinner. Instead, he surprises me.

"Let's walk," he says quietly, tilting his head toward the side corridor that leads out of the hotel.

I blink. "Walk?"

"The hotel has a private beach." His mouth curves, the faintest hint of a smile. "You like the ocean, don't you?"

Something tender unfurls in my chest. I nod, following him down the stone steps until sand spreads cool and fine beneath my heels. The waves crash in gentle rhythm, the horizon painted in fiery streaks as the sun begins to set.

I slip off my shoes and wander toward the water, dipping my toes into the surf. The tide curls around my ankles, warm and soothing. A breeze sweeps hair into my face, and before I can brush it aside, his fingers are there. Misha tucks the strands behind my ear, his knuckles grazing my cheek.

My breath catches.

We stand there, shoulder to shoulder, watching the sun sink lower.

"It's pretty," I murmur.

He hums in agreement, gaze fixed on the horizon.

And I think—this is it. This is the most romance I've ever been given. Not flowers handed out of obligation. Not empty words. But a night of good food, honest conversation, and a walk on the beach with the man I've wanted for years.

Victor could never give me this. He never tried. He only wanted the glitter of my fame, the satisfaction of conquest. But Mikhail, even with his walls and his wounds, is different. He doesn't treat me like a prize. He respects me. Even when he scares me, even when he pushes me away—there's care in him.

We settle into the sand, the waves whispering as the sky deepens into violet. I hug my knees, glancing at him, and nearly fall over when he asks, "Where do you want to go for our honeymoon?"

I stare. "Our... honeymoon?"

A laugh rumbles low in his chest, and it feels like the rarest of treasures. "What, you didn't think I'd take you somewhere? Leo will kill me if I don't."

I shake my head, still stunned. "I don't need anywhere

fancy. I'll be happy wherever you want to take me. I just... want to be with you."

His expression changes, softening, as though my words strike a place he doesn't want touched. For a second, I swear his eyes shine, glistening in the dying light. But no—that can't be. Mikhail doesn't cry. Probably sand carried by the wind.

"You're a good person," he says after a pause, voice rough. "You have terrible luck, though. Born into a Bratva household, marrying a villain like me."

My chest squeezes. I shake my head slowly. "I think villains are romantic."

That earns me a scoff, sharp but not cruel. "Romantic? What's romantic about villains?"

"They do things heroes won't," I say, lifting my gaze to his. "They'll cross lines, break rules, destroy anyone who threatens the people they love. And... they can be saved."

The words hang between us, quiet but unshakable, like the tide pressing at the shore.

He doesn't reply, but he doesn't need to. His silence speaks louder, echoing in the space between my heart and his.

And as I lean into the sound of the waves, one thought lodges deep inside me, stubborn and unmovable.

Maybe... I can save him from himself.

We stay on that beach for longer than we both intend. At some point, his hand settles over mine. I relish the weight of him, the subtle reminder that he's here, that he's with me.

But like all good things, our moment of connection and magic doesn't last forever. He gets a call and sighs. He gets up and I hope to my feet immediately.

He dusts off sand from my dress, curling his hand around my shoulder as he leads me back to the hotel, ear pressed to the phone. He speaks in Russian, and while I understand every word, I'm too busy focusing on how much I like his arm wrapped over me.

These subtle physical touches are new. He always avoided touching me before. But something changed in him after the night he took my virginity. He is generous with his touches now. Even at the dinner party, he touched my leg so many times.

But these touches are tender, more romantic. Less possessive and more loving. My heart flutters with every step we take.

I'm disappointed when we arrive at the door to my room. Our rooms are side by side. If I press my ear against the wall, maybe I'll hear his voice speaking in Russian on the other side.

But my girlish fantasies are brought to a swift end when he gestures at me to go inside my room and slips into his, waving with his hand.

No goodnight kiss. No lingering goodbye.

I sigh. Well, what did I expect? He probably got a really important call. Something must have come up in his business. Mikhail runs an empire worth millions. He doesn't have a lot of free time.

I slouch down on the bed, looking up at the ceiling.

When I touch my lips, I can still taste him. My pussy trembles, wanting his mouth. His tongue worked magic on my cunt last time. My legs were shivering when I came.

Tonight, I don't have his tongue, just my own fingers. I slide them under my waistband, caressing my swollen clit.

I'm wound up so tight, my muscles burst with fire the moment I tweak my clit. I run my fingers up and down my slick folds. My pussy leaks more moisture. I moan as my body is enveloped in a blanket of bliss.

It feels so good to let loose, to give myself the pleasure I need.

I test my pussy hole. It's slippery from arousal.

I'm so wet that my fingers slide easily between my folds, but it's not enough. It's never enough compared to him. I close my eyes, and I'm back there, back to the night he first took me. His hands weren't gentle then; they were demanding, bruising even, as he forced my legs apart. His eyes, dark and intense, held me captive as surely as his grip. I remember the shock of pain as he thrust into me, stealing my breath, my innocence. But then, oh God, then there was pleasure. A pleasure so intense it blurred the line between pain and ecstasy.

My fingers move faster, circling my clit, mimicking the rhythm he set that night. I recall his harsh breaths against my ear, the grunts that escaped him as he drove into me, again and again. The first orgasm had ripped through me unexpectedly, leaving me shuddering and gasping beneath him. But he didn't stop. He wrung another from me, forcing me to feel every inch of him, to take every punishing thrust until I was screaming his name, my body convulsing around his.

I cry, driving my fingers deep inside my channel. My pussy feels narrow yet tight when my walls clench around me, vibrating with desperate ache. I thrust in and out. Each slice of friction makes my belly contract, fans the heat in my core. Until it's a conflagration.

A fiery explosion I cannot contain. My veins surge with release, teetering on the brink of collapse. I push myself harder, even as I'm breathless. I draw big, noisy gulps of air, crying and moaning without shame every time I lodge my fingers inside my pussy.

I close my eyes as a ghostly pressure balloons inside me. Relief seems distant. But with a single curl of my fingers inside my pussy, at the same spot where Mikhail touched me, I clear the final hurdle.

I come with a long, loud wail, my back arching off the bed, my inner walls clenching around empty air. I can almost feel him, almost taste the ghost of his mouth on mine. But it's not the same. My fingers are a poor substitute for his thick cock, for the way he stretched me, filled me completely.

My breathing slows, my body still shivering with aftershocks. But there's an ache deep inside me, a hunger that hasn't been sated. I crave him, his weight on me, his scent enveloping me. I want the real thing, not this shadow of pleasure.

I withdraw my hand, my fingers slick with my release. I stare at them, remembering the sight of him, glistening with my virgin blood and his own desire. A brutal claim, a primal right. And yet, even then, there was something more. A connection, a bond forged in the heat of passion and pain.

A sigh escapes me as I roll over, burying my face in the pillow. It's not enough, it's never enough without him. Disappointment settles heavy in my chest, a gnawing emptiness that sleep can't fill. But I let the darkness take me, drift away on the memories of his touch, his kiss, his love. Maybe in my dreams, I'll find him again. Maybe there, he'll be truly mine.

THIRTEEN

MIKHAIL

Her moans haunt me all night. The echo of her passionate cries, the whisper of my name on her lips—it's a symphony of temptation that refuses to fade. I heard her, heard every whimper, every gasp as she pleasured herself, and it drove me mad. My cock throbbed, aching for her, and even after I cut my call short and stepped into the cold shower, jerking off to the thought of her, it wasn't enough. Her voice, her needy whimpers—they're branded into my mind, seducing me with every breath.

I wake up with a raging hard-on, a need so intense that it borders on pain. I need to see her, touch her. The need is so raw that I find myself texting her, asking her to come to my room for breakfast. My heart pounds as I wait, each second stretching into eternity.

When she finally arrives, she takes my breath away. She's in a lacy satin nightdress that clings to her curves, her breasts spilling over the top, nipples hard and teasing under the satin. She yawns, rubbing her tired eyes, her hair tousled and her face freshly washed. She looks so damn sexy that I can't stop myself.

I step closer, my hands reaching for her without conscious thought. I grope her breasts, feeling the weight of them in my palms, the hard peaks of her nipples under my fingers. She gasps, her eyes widening in surprise, but she doesn't pull away. I lean in, kissing and sucking on her neck, breathing in her scent. "You can't come around wearing stuff like this," I growl against her skin, "or I will have to put my cock inside your tight cunt and remind you how a modest Bratva wife should behave."

The threat wakes her up. She bites her lip, apologizing, and rushes back to her room. When she returns, she's tied a robe over her slinky nightdress. But it's too late—I've already seen her, ripe and delicious, her tits juicy enough to suck on for breakfast.

I touch her arm, leading her to the table where room service has laid out a spread. It has fruits, croissants, some eggs with sausage. Nothing grand. I know she's not a huge eater. Neither am I. I already drank coffee and that will help me power through the day. I have some important business deals to close in Miami. We're planning to expand our operations to the East Coast. There's no known cartel operating in this area, so it should be safe.

Zorina's lashes, full and beautiful, whisper against her cheek as she blinks, waiting for me to start.

I pinch her chin between my fingers, rubbing the smooth line of her jaw.

"Eat," I command, my voice rough with desire. She hesitates, and I raise an eyebrow. "Do I have to feed you?"

She still doesn't move. She's not scared. At least she doesn't look frightened. But I assume she has been taught at home to wait for a man to make the first move. Her father is traditional. Even on our dates, she waits for me to start eating before she does.

I take a cherry from the bowl and hold it to her lips.

"Open," I demand. She obeys, biting into the fruit, and the juices, red and lush, spray over my hand.

"Oh my God, I'm so sorry." Her cheeks go pink with embarrassment, but I'm turned on. The sight of her, her teeth biting into a cherry, the juices squirting down my palm, reminds me of her virgin blood smeared on my cock.

My groin buzzes with electricity. Fuck. I was meant to get my urges in control. But they flare up whenever she's around.

Zorina Morozova is a walking sin, one that I very much want to partake in.

"I'll wash my hands. Stay and eat." I rise before I get blue balls again and have to take another cold shower to calm down my raging hormones.

Once I'm in the bathroom, I run my hand under a cool spray of water. I dab away the moisture with a towel and stare at my reflection in the mirror. My pupils are dilated. I can feel my heart thudding.

I'm aroused.

I grip the marble counter in the bathroom, wondering what the hell I'm doing. Zorina is my weakness, a woman I can barely avoid pushing down and thrusting into, and yet here I am, inviting her into my room, where I could do anything to her.

Where I want to do everything to her.

I take deep breaths to compose myself. By the tenth, I'm feeling more in control.

But that control is short-lived. It disappears like a puff of smoke the moment I get back to my room and see whipped cream stuck to Zorina's cupid's bow.

My resistance crumbles. The fierce need from my cock threads through my veins, gripping my nerves, moving my limbs before I can reign it in.

"Such a fucking tease so early in the morning." I bite her earlobe, making her yelp. She loses her grip on the toast she's eating. It lands on her plate. "You have cream all over your lips, malyshka."

Cradling her face between my big, tattooed palms, I crush my mouth against hers. I suck on her lips, tracing her cupid's bow with the tip of my tongue, trying to get my fill of her. But even when I'm inside her mouth, exploring every inch of her sweetness, it's not enough.

This is all I can have before our wedding. The damn ceremony is more than six months away. Six months of restraining myself when all I want is to plunge into her soft heat every single night.

Her lips are soft beneath mine, sweeter than any wine, slick with need. I kiss her deeper, parting her mouth with my tongue, savoring every gasp. She clings to me, trembling, and when I finally take my mouth away, her pupils are blown wide.

She presses her thighs together, trying to hide what I already know—that she's wet, aching, just as helpless as I am.

"You've been... intense this morning," she whispers, her voice thin, uncertain. "Did I... did I do something wrong?"

I fall back into my chair with a sigh, dragging a hand down my face. She has no idea what she does to me. No idea how close I am to tearing through every vow of restraint.

"No," I rasp. "You didn't do anything wrong." I hesitate, then decide the truth is better than silence. "But I heard you last night, Zorina. When you were touching yourself."

Her whole body goes rigid. Color floods her face, her hands flying up to cover it.

A pitiful whimper escapes her throat. "Oh God... I can't— I can't face you."

"It's okay." I reach across the table, peeling her hands

gently from her face. "I don't mind. We can't touch each other the way we want, so this... this is the only way."

She shakes her head frantically, still refusing to meet my eyes. I growl low in my chest, drag her onto my lap, ignoring her squeak of surprise. My arm bands around her waist, my other hand stroking up and down her spine until she melts against me.

"My father would kill me if he found out," she cries out between deep breaths.

"It's okay," I murmur against her hair. "Your father isn't going to find out. And I won't kill you for wanting something everyone wants."

Her breath catches.

"Besides," I add with a crooked smile, tugging at her hand so she sees the diamond glinting on her finger, "you wear my ring. Vadim would think twice about killing my fiancée."

That finally earns me a smile, shy but real. "That... made me feel better."

I cup her jaw, brushing my thumb over her cheekbone. My voice softens. "You didn't do anything wrong."

"You don't think I'm a bad girl for touching myself?" Shock is visible on her features. I know her parents are more conservative than me. She must have grown up in a strict house, told to suppress her urges and her voice.

But I adore her fire, her boldness, her passion. It speaks to something within me. I enjoyed every single sound he made last night. My only regret is that I wasn't the one touching her.

"We're all evil, malyshka. Your father, me, everybody. We're in the bratva. We kill people, start wars, and turn humans into addicts. What right do we have to judge anybody?" I press my finger over her soft bottom lip. "A woman fingering herself isn't the most scandalous thing I've seen. You could say I have a different view good and bad."

She sniffs, her eyes filling with gratitude. "Thank you for being understanding. And forgiving me."

"There's nothing to forgive." But I can't leave it there. I lean closer, my lips ghosting over her ear. "Tell me, malyshka. Do you wish it had been me? Instead of your fingers?"

Her blush deepens. She breathes the word, fragile and fierce all at once. "Yes."

A sharp groan escapes me. My cock stiffens under her weight. "I've never lied about this. I'm physically attracted to you. You drive me insane. We can have sex before marriage, but I'd have to be careful. I'd have to use protection." I swallow hard, forcing the next words out. "Would you like that?"

She shakes her head, and for a heartbeat my chest hollows. I think she's refusing me.

But then she looks up through her lashes and whispers, "I don't want you to use protection. I loved feeling you the first time. I want that again."

Her words slam into me like a bullet. Heavy. Devastating. Her body feels significant on mine, her heat searing through my slacks. I'm left breathless by her confession, so raw and bold it strips me of my armor.

I'm ready to answer—ready to throw every plan into the fire —when my phone vibrates, the shrill ring breaking the spell.

"Fuck," I snarl, fishing it out of my pocket. A reminder flashes across the screen. My meeting. Miami business waits for no man, not even one drowning in lust for his fiancée.

Zorina slips off my lap, her cheeks flushed, her lips kiss-swollen, her whole body humming with the same torment I feel.

I stand, adjusting my jacket, my voice hoarse. "I have to go."

Her eyes follow me, wide, longing. And all I can think as I step away is that my control is hanging by a thread—and one day soon, it's going to snap.

THE BUSINESS MEETING DRAGS, my mind far from the polished men in suits and their promises about the East Coast. Expansion. Profit. Distribution routes. I nod at the right moments, keep my tone clipped, but inside I'm a storm.

All I can think about is her.

The way her body felt heavy on my lap. The way her voice broke when she whispered that she wanted me without protection. The way my cock is still aching, days later, with the memory of her tight around me.

I grit my teeth, scribble my signature, and push back from the table. The only solution when I get back is simple: lock myself in my room. Don't see her. Don't speak to her. Restraint is impossible otherwise.

But when I return to the hotel and knock on her door, there's no answer. Silence presses against me. I knock harder. Nothing.

A coil of unease tightens in my gut.

I glance out toward the beach through the glass lobby doors. The sand glimmers pale under the late afternoon sun. Empty.

Then I see it—the flash of blue water, the sound of laughter. The hotel pool sprawls just beyond the terrace, lined with white umbrellas and sun loungers. And there she is.

Zorina.

In a bikini that bares too much—creamy skin glowing, curves on display, her damp hair slicked back. My vision blurs with a red haze of possessiveness. Her hips are wide, perfect for bearing the babies I plan to put inside her. Her stomach is flat but not toned. But her tits are big and perky, pushing their way out of her halter-neck bikini top.

I storm out onto the pool deck, the humid air thick around me. The turquoise water glitters in the sunlight, children splash in the shallow end, waiters carry trays of cocktails garnished with fruit. None of it matters.

She's stretched out on a lounge chair, droplets clinging to her skin like diamonds. She looks like sin carved for me alone.

"What the hell are you doing?" My voice is rough, sharp enough to cut glass.

She startles, pushing her sunglasses up onto her hair. "Relaxing. What does it look like?"

"In next to nothing," I snap, my eyes raking down her body. "Prancing around, showing yourself to men who have no business seeing what's mine."

Her brows lift. "Prancing? I was swimming, Mikhail. That's what people do in Miami."

My fists clench. "Not you. Not like this."

Her mouth curves, teasing, but there's fire in her eyes. "So what do you want me to do? Sit locked in my room while you go to your meetings? Knit?"

"Don't test me," I growl.

"Why not?" she shoots back, tilting her head. "Because you don't like that other men look at me? Or because you don't like that I enjoy myself without you?"

Her words slam into me, sharp, precise, cutting through my restraint. I can feel eyes on us, men pretending not to stare, and it ignites every possessive instinct in me.

Enough.

I lunge forward, grab her wrist, and haul her up. She squeals, kicking, but I ignore it, slinging her over my shoulder like she weighs nothing.

"Put me down!" she protests, fists thumping against my back.

"No," I growl, striding across the pool deck, ignoring the gasps and curious stares we draw. "You want to know what kind of reaction that outfit inspires in men?" My palm cracks against the curve of her ass, a sharp smack that makes her gasp.

"Then I'll show you, malyshka. In private."

The fury in my chest mixes with heat, with need, until I can hardly tell them apart. I don't know if I want to lecture her, kiss her, or fuck her senseless.

Maybe all three.

Her fists thump against my back, her voice sharp with outrage. "Mikhail! Put me down this instant!"

I ignore her, stalking through the lobby and into the elevator. A couple gawks; one man dares to smirk. I level him with a glare so cold he drops his gaze immediately. Zorina squirms against me, but I only tighten my hold, my palm splayed possessively over the back of her thigh.

"Misha!" she calls me by the name only family uses, but I'm not softening.

"Shut up and stay still," I warn her.

I smack her ass when she continues to resist, beating her fists against my back. The other guests stare at us, but I don't care. She's mine and every fucker needs to know that.

When she knees me in the chest, I squeeze one ass cheek, growling. "Calm down, malyshka. Or I'll double your punishment. You won't be able to walk for the next two weeks. You cunt will be so sore from my cock that you'll barely sit without wincing. If that's what you want, keep going."

Zorina stops at once. Her arms hang over my shoulders, stilled. Satisfaction drips through me. I like how submissive she is, how eager she is to please me. And how she follows orders.

I knead her ass, priming her pussy to take me later. I don't have the patience for long drawn-out foreplay. She has had me on edge all day, thinking about what she said at breakfast.

Now it's time to make her pay for everything she has put my poor dick through.

The moans, the bold teasing, and the hourglass body that was created to shatter my self-control.

By the time we reach my room, her protests have dwindled into breathless whimpers. Not fear—never fear. But something else. Something molten.

I kick the door shut behind us and stride to the bedroom, dropping her onto the bed. She bounces against the white duvet, her hair tumbling wild around her flushed face.

"What the hell is wrong with you?" she snaps, pushing herself up on her elbows.

"You." My voice is gravel, low and dangerous. "Parading yourself half-naked where every man could see."

Her eyes flash, daring me. "I was swimming, Mikhail. What did you expect me to wear? A trench coat?"

The fire in her voice collides with the fire in my veins. I stalk closer, bracing a hand on the mattress, caging her in. "I expect you to remember you're mine. That every curve, every inch of you belongs to me alone."

She leans up, close enough that our mouths almost touch. "Then maybe you should start acting like I'm yours. Instead of avoiding me every time we get close to having sex."

My restraint snaps.

I seize her mouth with mine, crushing my lips against hers. It isn't tender this time—it's brutal, hungry, the kind of kiss that leaves bruises. She gasps, and I take the opening, thrusting my tongue inside, claiming her sweetness.

Her hands fly to my shoulders, nails digging into muscle, pulling me closer instead of pushing me away. The bikini is damp, clinging to her curves, and when my palm skims over her hip, it's like touching liquid fire.

I growl against her mouth. "This is what you do to me, malyshka. This is why I can't let anyone else look at you. Your body could make a man lose his reason."

She presses her thighs together, her breath hot against my lips. "And what are you going to do about it?"

My fingers slip under the thin string at her waist, tugging it hard enough to make her gasp. My mouth trails down her throat, biting, sucking, marking her skin. "I'm going to remind you why no other man gets to imagine what's under this. Only me."

Her whimper nearly undoes me. My cock aches, hard and heavy against the zipper of my slacks. Every instinct screams to tear the bikini off her and sink inside until she's screaming my name.

But I force myself to pause, my forehead pressing against hers, my breath ragged.

"If I don't stop now," I grind out, "there won't be a damn thing left of my control."

Her eyes, wide and dilated, lock on mine. She licks her lips. "Then don't stop."

Her words shatter the last of my restraint. A primal growl tears from my throat as I grip the strings of her bikini, yanking them hard. The fabric gives way, exposing her to me, and I drink in the sight of her—flushed skin, heaving breasts, nipples hard and begging for my mouth.

I push her back onto the bed, my body covering hers, pinning her down. My mouth crashes against hers again, our teeth clashing, tongues clashing in a wild dance of dominance and submission. She moans into my mouth, her nails raking down my back, and I growl in approval.

"That's it, malyshka," I rasp against her lips. "Show me how much you want this. How much you want me."

I move down her body, my mouth tracing a heated path over her skin. I capture one nipple in my mouth, sucking hard, making her arch off the bed with a cry. My hand finds her other breast, squeezing, pinching, drawing out a gasp from deep within her.

"Misha," she whimpers, her voice breathy and desperate. "Please..."

"Please what?" I demand, releasing her nipple with a pop. "What do you want, Zorina?"

Her eyes flutter open, hazy with desire. "I want you inside me. I want you to take me, to make me yours."

A dark, possessive smile curves my lips. "Oh, you're already mine, malyshka. That's why you must be punished. Because you forgot what it meant to be mine."

I grip her hips, flipping her onto her stomach before pulling her back onto her knees. She gasps, her hands fisting the sheets, her ass in the air, presented to me like an offering. I run my hand over the curve of her ass, savoring the softness, the heat.

"Spread your legs. Show me that slutty cunt that you tried to show other men" I command, my voice rough with need.

She obeys instantly, her thighs parting, revealing her glistening pussy. I groan at the sight, my cock throbbing with the urge to be inside her.

I trace her fast pussy lips. "Your bikini was clinging to your pussy like it was painted onto it. I could see the swell of your pussy lips. And so did everyone else."

I slap her pussy. She cries out, but she takes her punishment without protest. Like a good girl. Like a good bratva wife.

Thinking of her as my wife births a storm inside my groin. My cock tightens with heat. My balls feel heavy with seed I need to unload inside her before I explode.

But first, I want to taste her. I want to drink her in, to drown in her sweetness. I have waited to do this again for so long.

I dip my head, my tongue licking a long, slow path up her slit. She shivers, a moan escaping her lips. I do it again, this time lingering at her clit, circling the sensitive bud, drawing out a gasp from deep within her.

"Misha," she whimpers, her hips bucking against my mouth. "Please, don't tease me. I'm going to burst."

She's not lying. Her legs are quivering like a leaf in a storm. She's shaking from the force of her own arousal as clear streams run down her thighs, showing me how needy she is for my cock.

Her words send a bolt of lust through me. I straighten up, my hands gripping her hips, my cock poised at her entrance.

I drive into her, hard and deep, filling her completely. She cries out, her body tensing around me, her inner walls clamping down on my cock.

"Fuck," I growl, the sensation almost too much to bear. "You're so tight, so perfect."

I pull back, then thrust into her again, my hips slamming against her ass. She moans, her fingers clawing at the sheets, her body writhing beneath me. I set a brutal pace, pounding into her, each thrust driving her deeper into the mattress.

"Is this what you wanted, malyshka?" I grunt, my fingers digging into her hips. "To be taken, to be fucked raw and hard?"

"Yes," she gasps, her voice barely audible. "Yes, Misha, please..."

I lean forward, my body covering hers, my mouth at her ear. "Your punishment for betraying me will be carrying my baby when you get married," I growl, my voice low and dark. "Everyone will whisper, but I'll hold your swollen belly, reminding you just how you got it as I slip my ring onto your finger."

She shivers beneath me, a moan of pure, unadulterated desire escaping her lips. "Yes, Misha. Breed me. Make me yours."

Her words send me into a frenzy. I thrust into her harder, deeper, my grip on her hips bruising. She meets each thrust with a cry, her body trembling, her pussy clenching around my cock.

Her breasts bounce with every deep stroke, responding to me. I love watching her tits jiggling as I plow into her, grabbing her hair now, riding her like I own her.

"You're going to take every stroke, malyshka. Until your pussy is screaming to come. Until you're hurting so much, you'll be sore all day."

She pulls her head back, moaning, but I'm not unnecessarily brutal. I don't yank her hair hard. My hands venture lower. I curl my fingers around her breasts for support, squeezing them, rubbing her taut nipples with my thumbs. Her pussy releases more moisture, coating my cock, easing my path.

"That's it, malyshka," I rasp, my breath hot against her ear. "Take my cock. Take my seed. Take everything I give you. That's your punishment."

Her body tightens around me, her breath coming in short, sharp gasps. I can feel her orgasm building, her inner walls fluttering, her muscles tensing. I reach around, my fingers finding her clit, rubbing it in quick, tight circles.

"Come for me, Zorina," I command, my voice rough with need. "Come all over my cock. Show me how much you love being bred by me."

Her body convulses, her orgasm ripping through her. She screams my name, her pussy clamping down on my cock, her juices flooding around me. The sensation sends me over the edge, my own release exploding from me. I bury myself deep inside her, my cock pulsing, my seed filling her, claiming her, breeding her.

I spray my seed all over her fertile, unprotected walls. Load after load. Until my balls are drained and I'm satisfied. All the pent-up frustration I've held for days flows into her pussy, filling her to the brim. Until she starts dripping sticky semen like a cumslut.

"It's not over yet." I push my cum back inside her with my

fingers, making sure it stays inside her fertile heat. "You're going to keep my seed warm inside you until it starts growing in your womb. Your punishment is not over yet, Zorina."

Her eyes are innocent and trusting when she looks up at me. It melts a hard wall inside me. She looks like an angel, lying on the white sheets, my cum oozing out of her freshly-fucked pussy.

I can't give her all of myself, not yet, but I can give her enough to keep her full of me all night.

FOURTEEN

Zorina

THE FIRST THING I notice when I wake is the weight. Heavy, warm, inescapable.

Mikhail's arm is banded across my waist, his hand splayed wide over my stomach like he's staking a claim even in sleep. One of his powerful legs is hooked over my hip, keeping me pinned to the bed, pressed flush against his chest. His body is a cage and a shelter all at once, and for the first time in my life, I don't want to escape.

I shift slightly, and a dull ache radiates through my thighs, between my legs. Soreness lingers everywhere, a constant reminder of what happened last night—his fury, his hunger, his relentless drive to prove that I was his. My body feels branded, marked inside and out.

But even beneath the memory of his punishment, I feel safe. Protected. Wanted.

My gaze lingers on his face in the soft morning light spilling through the curtains. Without the hard mask of control, he looks so different. His lashes lie dark against his skin, his lips parted, his features unguarded. Peaceful. Vulnerable. It's a face no one else will ever see.

Carefully, I lift my hand, tracing the bridge of his nose with the tip of my finger, then the bow of his lips. I linger at his lashes, marveling at how long they are, how unfairly beautiful. For these few moments, while he sleeps, he's mine. Like his heartbeat in my palm, his peace belongs to me.

I try to ease out from under him, but he stirs, pulling me tighter, his voice gravelly and thick with sleep. "Too early," he grumbles, burying his face in my hair. "Not letting you go."

A laugh escapes me, hushed and shaky. "Don't you have a meeting?"

He groans, the sound vibrating through my back. "I do. But I just want to stay tangled up in you."

My heart swells at that. This—this is the Mikhail no one else knows. The man who clings, who wants. Not the Pakhan's brother, not the Bratva businessman. Just a man in bed with the woman he can't seem to let go of.

"I don't mind staying," I whisper.

His mouth brushes over my cheek, then lingers on mine. The kiss is soft, almost reverent. When he pulls back, his thumb strokes across my jaw, tender. "You look beautiful."

Heat rushes through me. "What you did to me last night might have something to do with it," I tease.

He chuckles, low and dark, before his expression softens again. His hand trails down my side, over the curve of my hip, settling gently between my thighs. "Are you sore?" he asks, his tone hushed, careful.

I nod, biting my lip. "A little."

He presses a kiss to my forehead, then another to my

temple. His fingers trace light, soothing circles along my hip. "I was too rough. I should've—"

"No." I shake my head quickly, cutting him off. "Don't apologize. I... liked it. All of it."

He exhales, his breath hot against my skin, and tucks me even closer. "Still. You're mine to protect, not break."

A lump rises in my throat. In his arms, cocooned like this, I believe him. Whatever he does to me, whatever we become, I will always feel safe here.

We trade soft kisses until he pulls back and says, "What do you want for breakfast?"

I blink, thrown by the normalcy of it. "You're giving me choices?"

His lips twitch. "Always. Tell me, malyshka. Eggs? Pancakes? Fruit?"

"Croissants," I whisper. "And maybe strawberries."

"Done." He picks up the phone, his voice brisk as he orders from room service. Watching him—this powerful, dangerous man—make sure I get the exact breakfast I want makes me laugh.

"You're spoiling me."

His thumb brushes my lower lip. "Get used to it. You're going to be a rich man's wife soon. You should feel spoiled."

I laugh, tucking myself into his chest, inhaling the faint trace of his cologne still clinging to his skin. "I feel... luxurious. Like this isn't my life. Like I borrowed someone else's."

He studies me. "Why?"

Because mine was never like this. The words spill out before I can stop them. "Even though I grew up in a Bratva family, I was always given so little. My father thought indulgence made people weak. Even my violin—the one he bought me—was second-hand. He didn't want me wasting time on hobbies. It was like he was afraid I'd become too good at something outside his world."

Mikhail's hand stills against my back. His eyes are fierce, protective.

"I bought a new one later," I go on, my throat tight. "After I sold some of my clothes. The old one held me back. I was advancing so fast... I needed better. So I made it happen."

He leans in, kissing the corner of my mouth, his voice raw. "You've been so brave." His lips find mine again, slower this time. "You'll never have to beg me for a violin. Or for anything."

Tears sting my eyes, but I smile instead, cupping his cheek. "You gave me more than a violin, Misha. You gave me the chance to live my dreams."

His forehead rests against mine, his eyes closed. For a man who has spent his whole life wielding control like a weapon, he suddenly looks undone by my words.

And for the first time, I realize: last night wasn't just punishment. It was possession. And this morning—this tenderness, this aftercare—is proof of something even more dangerous.

That he might not be as unfeeling as he believes.

THE DAY STRETCHES OUT like an empty canvas, waiting for him to return.

I curl up on the sofa with a novel, but after a few pages my mind drifts—back to Mikhail's arms around me this morning, to his lips brushing mine, to the ache that still lingers between my thighs. I try to practice, pulling out sheet music and setting bow to string, but my body betrays me. Each note trembles with distraction, the soreness tugging my thoughts back to the way he took me, the way he soothed me afterward.

By late afternoon, I give up and return to my room, frustrated with myself. I want him. I miss him. And I hate that the hours without him feel so long.

The phone on my nightstand rings.

I glance at the caller ID and my stomach dips. Mama.

I take a breath, press accept. "Hello."

"Zorina," her voice is sharp, brisk, already full of judgment. "Are you keeping his interest?"

I bite my lip. "I... think so."

As if that's something measurable, like practicing scales. Maybe I should file a report: *Dear Mama, yes, I pleased the Bratva man today. Gold star for me.*

"And what are you wearing to the gala tomorrow?"

"I don't know yet."

She clucks her tongue. "You must. Plan it. Wear something that makes him proud. Elegant, but not too flashy. Let him shine. You must be quiet, submissive. Let him feel like the man."

My jaw tightens. "I understand."

What I *want* to say is: If you knew Mikhail, you'd know he doesn't need my silence to feel like a man.

But then she says it. The words that make my blood boil.

"You must turn a blind eye to his affairs. They all stray. Don't be foolish. And if he ever strikes you, don't speak up. Endure. That is the way of our world."

The room tilts. My pulse pounds in my ears.

"He won't," I snap, voice shaking. "And if he ever does, I won't be staying. Not for anyone. Not for anything."

"Don't be emotional. Be sensible," Mama insists. "Violence is commonplace. A woman cannot live alone."

"Yes, I can," I shoot back. "I'm a successful violinist. I have enough money to live on my own—"

"No, you don't," she interrupts, voice rising. "You need a man to protect you."

The words scrape raw against my chest, years of old-fashioned chains tightening all at once.

"No, I don't!" I scream, my voice cracking.

The door clicks open.

I turn, my breath catching.

Mikhail stands in the doorway, filling it with his broad frame. His tie is gone, his collar unbuttoned, his dark stubble shadowing his jaw. He looks hot in that devastating, dangerous way that makes my knees weak.

I end the call abruptly, the dial tone humming in the silence.

He's already striding toward me. "What's wrong?" His hands close over my arms, his touch grounding, firm. "Zorina. Are you okay?"

My eyes sting. "Mama. She was... being annoying."

His gaze sharpens. "What did she say?"

I hesitate, biting my lip. I don't want to repeat it.

His hand slides up and down my back, soothing, coaxing. "You can tell me. I'm used to your opinions by now. I've been with you for six years, malyshka."

The words loosen something in me. My eyes lock with his. "She said... she said I should take it if you hit me." My voice shakes, but I steady it. "But I won't. And I meant it. I'm not going to be abused by any man."

His face hardens, but not with anger at me. His arms pull me into his chest, crushing me close. "I don't expect you to," he says fiercely. "Only pathetic men hit their wives to feel strong. I'll never take out my anger on you."

The vow reverberates through me, settling deep. I cling to him, fisting his suit jacket. Safe. I feel safe.

He's breaking open a part of me that I've always protected. I've always tried to remain independent emotionally, never leaning on anybody to feel better or safer. I knew I was alone in the world. I now realize I had to be become independent because the people around me were not emotionally comforting anyway.

I never had someone like this. Someone who'd listen to me, someone who'd hold my anger, hold me and make me feel like I'm heard. I'm seen. I'm right.

Depending on Mikhail, letting him soothe me, letting him calm down my anger and irritation at the world is a balm I never knew I needed.

I want him to stay, not leave. I want to remain in his embrace, soaking up his solidity and assurance. Letting him ground me and dissolve the rage inside me.

It feels like I finally have an ally in the unyielding bratva world. Someone who will support me, defend me. And it's so weird that it's my arranged marriage fiancé.

His hand drifts lower to the small of my back, rubbing. A shot of electricity zaps my pussy. I feel the trickle of moisture, but also the ache from last night's intense lovemaking. I'm still not completely healed. I can't take his huge cock tonight. It will destroy me.

"Misha," I whisper. "I can't... I can't make love tonight. I'm still sore."

His lips brush my hair. "I expected that. Conserve your energy. Tomorrow is the gala. Your dress will be delivered in the morning, and I've arranged a personal makeup artist."

The way he says it, calm, thoughtful, sends warmth through me. He's thinking of me. He's planning for me.

I tip my face up to him, trying for a smile. "Then tonight...

can we just watch a movie? Something innocent. To take my mind off her."

He nods, surprising me. "That sounds good. I've had a tough day. I need some escapism, too."

On the couch, he pulls me into his lap before I can sit beside him. I wriggle. "Misha—"

"I like you here." His hand spreads across my thigh, heavy and possessive. "Where you belong."

Heat creeps into my cheeks. But the truth? I like it too. I curl against him, pressing play on a Disney movie of all things, the bright colors flickering across the room.

I expect him to launch a protest, but he seems engrossed in the movie. Who knew a scary bratva businessman like Mikhail Antonov would be into children's animated movies? I smile, loving this unexpectedly cute side of him.

His hand stays on me, not urgent, just steady. And I feel... cozy.

I never thought I'd be here, tucked into Mikhail Antonov's lap, watching a cartoon about princesses and magic. But maybe his strength, his warmth, his presence is its own kind of fairytale.

And for once, I let myself believe in it.

FIFTEEN

Mikhail

THE SUITE DOOR OPENS, and for a moment, I forget how to breathe.

She steps out, the silk of the gown whispering over the carpet, clinging to her curves like it was painted onto her body. The dress is a deep sapphire blue, plunging low at the back, the fabric catching every flicker of light until she looks as though she's walking through starlight itself. Her hair is swept up, stray curls brushing her neck, her skin glowing under the chandelier.

Zorina. My fiancée. My future wife.

She bites her lip, watching me watch her. "Too much?"

I cross the room in three strides, seize her hand, and kiss her hard, claiming her mouth with no room for doubt. She sways against me, gasping softly when I pull back.

"Perfect," I rasp. "I'm proud to have you on my arm tonight."

Her eyes widen. "Because I'm pretty?"

I shake my head, my thumb brushing over her knuckles. "No. Because I'm certain you'll be the most accomplished partner at the gala. You're not just a pretty face, Zorina. You're talent. You're fire. And they'll all see it."

Something blooms in her expression—light, joy, pride. She glows brighter than the gown itself. "Thank you," she whispers. "For seeing me beyond the surface."

"How can I not see?" I murmur, cupping her jaw. "You're so bright, malyshka. I can't take my eyes off you."

Her smile could set the world aflame. I slide my hand around her waist, guiding her out of the suite. She fits against me perfectly, and the click of her heels on marble echoes like a countdown to something inevitable.

In the car, her hand rests on mine, warm and certain. I almost forget about business, about enemies, about everything beyond this moment.

Then my phone vibrates. Leo.

I swipe to answer. "What is it?"

"Nikolai will be coming over after New Year," my brother says. "He'll spend some time with you. He's bringing a new friend. Clara."

I blink. "Nikolai made a friend?"

"Yes," Leo says dryly. "Miracles happen."

I grunt. "We'll see how long she lasts."

There's a pause, then Leo's tone shifts. "You've been treating Zorina well, I hope?"

"Yes," I answer without hesitation.

"Good. Put her on."

I glance at her. She's already giggling, reaching for the phone. Against my better judgment, I give it to her.

"Leo," she says, laughter bubbling in her voice, "Mikhail has been fulfilling all my fantasies. I can't even believe he's the same man as before."

My jaw tightens, heat flooding my chest—not anger, not embarrassment, but something far more dangerous. She's teasing me, but she's also telling the truth.

Leo chuckles on the other end. "Glad to hear you're not planning to elope before the wedding."

I snatch the phone back. "Are you happy now?"

"Very," Leo says, laughter in his voice. "I'm glad you're having fun in Miami, brother."

"I'm here for business," I snap. "And the business is dealt with."

"I know," Leo says, the amusement still there.

I hang up, sliding the phone into my pocket. Beside me, Zorina leans her head against my shoulder.

I don't move. I don't stop her.

In fact, I like it. I like her weight there, her warmth seeping into me. And though I don't say it, I think it: I could get used to this.

THE GALA IS all glitter and noise, chandeliers dripping with crystal, champagne flutes catching the light like prisms. Every table is covered in white linen, the air heavy with perfume, cigar smoke, and the hum of Russian and English voices overlapping in a symphony of wealth and power.

And then there's Zorina.

Her breasts are full and bouncy, jiggling with every movement. Her ass bounces, plump and huge. She's a femme fatale, and every man in the room notices. Heads turn as she walks in on my arm. Their gazes linger too long—on the dip of her back, on the curve of her breasts—and pride and fury burn in me at the same time.

She's friendly, smiling warmly at every man who

approaches, laughing softly when they compliment her, speaking to them with that bright light that makes her irresistible. I know she's doing it for me, for us—for the alliance—but I want to rip every man's eyes out.

I tighten my hand on her wrist, pulling her subtly closer. I lean down, my lips brushing her ear. "Careful, malyshka. You smile so sweetly, so prettily, I might not be able to resist devouring you the second we're back at the hotel."

She swallows hard, her throat bobbing.

"Are you still sore?" I murmur, my hand sliding down to brush the silk at her waist. "Be honest."

She looks up at me, eyes bright with mischief. "No. I'm not. And I'm looking forward to all your possessiveness in bed later."

My breath stutters. I freeze, realization dawning. I draw back just enough to see her smug, teasing smile. "You didn't."

Her laugh is light, wicked. "I did. Triggering your jealousy is the only way to get any intimacy from you."

Heat flashes through me—anger, arousal, amusement all tangled together. I sling my arm around her shoulders, pulling her tight against me so no one else can even look at her. "There are other ways, too."

She tilts her head. "Like what?"

I smirk, lowering my voice so only she hears. "You could show up at my apartment naked. Or send me nude photos. I'd clear my schedule for that."

Her cheeks flush crimson, her lips parting. The image clearly shocks her—and excites her.

"I always want you, Zorina," I tell her, serious now. "You don't have to try so hard."

"But you hold yourself back," she says softly, a little frown pulling at her mouth. "You stop yourself from doing anything."

My jaw tightens. She's right.

"I don't want to take too much from you," I admit, the words grating against my pride.

She shakes her head, her hand slipping into mine, her voice fierce. "I'm yours. You can take whatever you want."

Her certainty stuns me. Her willingness. Her giving heart. She doesn't even realize it, but she's always offering more of herself than she should—her time, her music, her body, her soul.

And I realize then, under the chandeliers and the curious eyes of the Bratva, that I don't just want to take. I want to protect that generosity. To keep it from being consumed by anyone else, even me.

SIXTEEN

Zorina

THE RIDE back to the hotel passes in a blur of city lights and the heavy press of Mikhail's arm around me. My pulse beats faster with every second, anticipation thrumming in my veins. When the elevator doors close behind us, sealing us in, I can feel his heat, his nearness, the restrained hunger in every breath he takes.

By the time we step into the suite, I'm trembling with it.

He doesn't pounce. He doesn't rush. Instead, he circles me slowly, like a predator savoring the sight of its prey. His eyes darken as they travel down the sapphire gown that had so many men staring tonight.

"Turn around," he orders softly.

My breath hitches as I do. His hands, steady and warm, slide up my back, finding the clasp. With a soft click, the gown loosens, the silk gliding down my body until it pools at my feet in a whisper.

He presses a kiss to my bare shoulder. "You did so well tonight. Your first outing as my fiancée. You handled it perfectly." His lips trail to my neck, each word sending shivers down my spine. "I can't wait to take you to more parties once you're Mrs. Antonova."

The name makes me shiver all over again. Mrs. Antonova. To belong to him fully, publicly, permanently. To be tied not only to him but to his family, the family that has already shown me more acceptance, more warmth, than my own ever has.

Mikhail's brothers see me. They ask about my career. They tease me like I belong. And he—this impossible, flawed, extraordinary man—he puts every hero I've ever read about in my romance novels to shame.

"What are you thinking, malyshka?" he murmurs, his lips brushing the shell of my ear.

I bite my lip, daring to whisper the truth. "I'm wondering... what you'll do to me."

He chuckles low, dark, delicious. "That's a surprise. And I want you to discover it slowly."

He guides me to the bed, seating me on the edge. From the silver tray left by room service, he plucks a strawberry, its skin glossy and red. He holds it to my lips, his eyes never leaving mine.

"Open."

My lips part. He brushes the fruit against them, then slides it between, watching intently as my teeth sink into the sweetness, the juice spilling over my tongue. His thumb catches a droplet at the corner of my mouth, rubbing it slowly into my skin before lifting his finger to his lips and licking it clean.

"You taste better than this," he says huskily, leaning down to kiss me, the faint tang of strawberry mixing with the warmth of his mouth.

His hands are everywhere, stroking down my arms,

cupping my breasts, sliding lower over my stomach, his touch reverent but demanding. He kisses me again, deeper this time, until I'm dizzy with him.

"You're mine," he whispers against my lips. "Every smile, every sigh, every sound you make tonight will belong to me and no one else."

And as he lowers me gently back against the pillows, feeding me strawberries one by one, showering me with kisses and praises, I think to myself: this isn't just seduction. It's worship.

And God help me, I want to be worshipped by him forever.

This is so different from the sex we've had before. It's not rough, intense, or hurried. It's slow and careful, like he wants to relish every second we get to spend together. Like this time together means something to him.

I can sense the way things have shifted between us during this trip. We'll be going back home tomorrow, and I'll have to bury myself in recordings, composition, and rehearsals again. My heart stings at the thought that this intimacy might disappear, that we might go back to our own worlds and stop seeing each other once we're back.

"Can we keep doing this once we're back in Las Vegas?" I beg.

"That depends on how you do tonight." Misha presses a firm kiss to my belly. "Come for me twice. Then I'll think about it."

His smile tells me he's playing with me, but this new level of affection from him is so fragile, I'm afraid of losing it.

His lips brush against the skin just beneath my navel, and I shiver with anticipation. Mikhail's eyes, dark and intense, meet mine as he slowly begins to peel off my clothes, his fingers tracing every curve and line of my body as if it were a sacred ground. Each touch is deliberate, each kiss a claim of ownership.

"Every inch of you is mine, Zorina," he murmurs, his breath hot against my skin. "Now I want to see my pretty fiancée orgasm for me."

He unhooks my bra, freeing my breasts, and I gasp as his mouth finds one nipple, suckling deeply. His tongue flicks against the hardened peak, sending jolts of pleasure straight to my core. I arch into him, needing more, always more. He moves to the other breast, lavishing it with the same attention, his teeth grazing the sensitive flesh, drawing out a moan from deep within me.

"Misha," I whisper, my fingers tangling in his hair, pulling him closer. "Please..."

He chuckles, a low, dark sound that vibrates through me. "Patience, malyshka. I want to savor you."

His mouth trails lower, kissing every part of me as if it were a ground to be worshipped. He lingers at the dip of my waist, the curve of my hip, the soft skin of my inner thigh. I tremble under his touch, my body aching with need.

When he finally reaches my pussy, he pauses, his breath hot against my sensitive flesh. He looks up at me, his eyes filled with a hunger that makes my heart race. "This is mine," he growls, his voice possessive and dominant. "Every drop of your pleasure belongs to me."

His tongue delves into my folds, licking and tasting, exploring every inch of me. I cry out, my hips bucking against his mouth as waves of pleasure crash over me. He sucks on my clit, his fingers sliding into me, curling and stroking until I'm panting and begging for release.

"Come for me, Zorina," he commands, his voice rough with desire. "Let me hear you scream in pleasure."

My body obeys, convulsing around his fingers as the first

orgasm rips through me. I scream his name, my hands fisting the sheets, my body shaking with the force of my release.

But Mikhail isn't done with me yet. He flips me onto my stomach, his hands gripping my hips as he pulls me up onto my knees. I feel the head of his cock, hot and hard, pressing against my entrance.

"I'm going to fuck you now," he growls, his voice filled with a primal need. "I'm going to breed you, fill you with my seed until you're dripping with it."

He thrusts into me, hard and deep, his cock stretching and filling me completely. I cry out, the sensation overwhelming, the pleasure and pain merging into one exquisite sensation. He sets a brutal pace, his hips slamming against mine, his fingers digging into my flesh.

"You feel so good," he rasps, his breath hot against my ear. "I want to stay inside you all night, keep breeding you until you're unmistakably the mother of my child."

His words send me spiraling, my body tightening around him, my second orgasm building with every thrust. He reaches around, his fingers finding my clit, rubbing tight circles until I'm gasping and writhing beneath him.

"Come for me again," he demands, his voice rough with need. "Come all over my cock. Milk me, Zorina. Take every drop of my seed."

My body convulses, the second orgasm even more intense than the first. I scream his name, my inner walls clamping down on his cock, my juices flooding around him. He groans, his body tensing as he finds his own release, his cock pulsing deep inside me, filling me with his hot, thick seed.

But even as our bodies slow, he doesn't pull out. Instead, he flips me onto my back, his cock still buried deep inside me. He lifts my legs, hooking my ankles over his shoulders, and begins to move again, slower this time, his eyes locked onto mine.

"I want to see you," he murmurs, his voice soft yet commanding. "I want to watch your face as you come for me again."

His thrusts are deep and deliberate, each one hitting a spot inside me that sends waves of pleasure coursing through my veins. His hands roam over my body, cupping my breasts, pinching my nipples, his touch both gentle and possessive.

"You're mine," he whispers, his eyes filled with a dark intensity. "Every part of you belongs to me. Your smiles, your laughter, your tears—all mine."

His words fill me with a warmth that goes beyond the physical pleasure. It's a sense of belonging, of being cherished, that I've never felt before. And as the third orgasm builds, I know that I'm lost to him completely.

"Misha," I gasp, my body tensing, my breath coming in short, sharp bursts. "I... I'm going to come again."

He leans down, his lips brushing against mine, his breath mingling with my own. "Come for me, malyshka," he murmurs. "Show me how much your body craves me. I'm the only man who can make you orgasm like this. Remember that."

And with one final, deep thrust, he sends me over the edge. My body convulses around him, my third orgasm ripping through me, leaving me breathless and shaking.

His cock twitches inside me. Then his cum is painting my walls, flooding my channel with potent seed. I take every drop he unloads inside me. His cock pumps load after load into my receptive, fertile pussy, filling me to the brim.

"Good girl." His praise only prolongs the haze from my orgasm. He kisses my cheek, collapsing next to me, slinging his arm over my body. "And yes, we'll be having sex even after we get back. Maybe not at this pace, though. You tire me out, malyshka. Your pussy wrings everything from my cock."

I skim my fingers over his skin, his body slick with sweat,

his breath ragged. All I can think about is how good it feels to have him inside me. How right it feels to be claimed by him, to be his completely.

And as I drift off into sleep, wrapped in his arms, I know that whatever happens when we go back to Las Vegas, this connection, this intimacy, is worth fighting for. Because Mikhail Antonov isn't just the man I'm going to marry. He's the man who has claimed every part of me, body and soul. And I am his, forever.

LAS VEGAS FEELS different after Miami. The dry desert heat presses against me as I step out of the car each morning, and the neon skyline never sleeps, but none of it compares to the ocean air or the way Mikhail made me feel when he whispered I was his.

I throw myself into the studio, drowning in melodies. My violin becomes my confessor, the bow my voice. I scribble down notes for my next album, determined to make something raw and beautiful. Still, I check my phone between takes more often than I should.

Mikhail's texts are waiting, always.

Misha: Did you eat lunch?

I roll my eyes, smiling as I type back:

Me: No. I'm living on the sound of your voice in my head.

His reply is instant.

Misha: That explains why you're still so skinny.

Me: You could say *romantic* things instead of sarcastic quips, you know.

Misha: You knew what you signed up for.

I laugh, shoving the phone into my pocket, only to pull it out again an hour later.

Misha: Did you get home safe?

I sigh. He's back to the usual questions—the ones that used to make our engagement feel like a polite business transaction instead of what it became in Miami. My chest tightens with a strange fear.

Are we slipping back into the cold arrangement we had before? Was Miami just a dream?

I remember his words that last night, his voice rough in my ear, telling me there were other ways to get his attention. Naked in his apartment. Nude pictures. My cheeks burn at the memory.

Before I can overthink, I'm moving.

I shower, towel my hair, spray a touch of perfume at my wrists. Then I shrug into a long beige coat—nothing else underneath. The silk lining whispers against bare skin, making me shiver as I step into the elevator that carries me up to his penthouse.

My heart thuds as I knock.

The door swings open. He stands there, broad-shouldered, devastating in a black shirt with the sleeves rolled up, veins visible on his forearms. His eyes narrow, then widen.

"Zorina." His voice is startled, suspicious. "What are you doing here?"

I tilt my head, feigning nonchalance, though my pulse is racing. "Are you busy?"

"No." His gaze flicks behind me. "Is someone with you?"

"No one."

"Good." I smile, sliding one hand to my coat. "Because I'm not wearing anything."

His pupils blow wide. I pop the first few buttons open. Silk lining parts, exposing bare flesh, the swell of my breasts catching the light.

His sharp inhale is audible, dragging the air between us taut as a bowstring.

The silence between us stretches, heavy and electric. His gaze is fixed on the opening of my coat, on the inch of bare skin revealed with each undone button. His throat works, his jaw tightening like he's wrestling with himself.

I smile sweetly, even as my heart pounds like a drum. "What's wrong, Misha? Cat got your tongue?"

His eyes snap to mine, dark, sharp, molten. "You're playing with fire."

I slip another button open, the fabric parting wider. Cool air rushes against my stomach. "Maybe I like fire."

His nostrils flare. He steps closer, slow, deliberate, his body towering over mine. "Do you have any idea what you're doing?"

"Yes," I whisper, tilting my chin up. "I'm seducing you. And judging by your face, it's working."

A low growl vibrates in his chest. "You're shameless."

"And you like it," I shoot back, letting the coat fall just enough to show the curve of my hip. "Don't you?"

That's the crack in his armor.

He surges forward, one hand gripping my wrist, the other slamming flat against the wall beside my head. The force of it makes my breath hitch, my back pressing to the cool surface. His body cages mine in, heat rolling off him in waves.

"You think you can walk into my apartment naked under a coat," he growls, his mouth inches from mine, "and I'll just stand here and do nothing?"

I bite my lip, meeting his gaze head-on. "That was the plan."

His control snaps like glass under a hammer.

With a savage curse, he shoves the coat open, baring me

completely. His eyes rake down, slow and scorching, drinking me in. His chest rises and falls in ragged breaths, and then his mouth crashes onto mine. Hard, punishing, devouring.

The wall vibrates with the force of it, my body arching into his, heat sparking everywhere his hands touch.

And in that instant, I know: the man who once kept me at arm's length is gone. The one before me now is fire and hunger and possession, and I've set him free.

Mikhail unleashes every ounce of restrained passion as his mouth plunders mine, robbing every sigh and moan of pleasure from me. All these years, when I saw him sitting at my concerts, watching me with cool, assessing eyes, I never would have predicted he was hiding such explosive passion underneath.

I know his cousin's death scarred him, made him unwilling to love a woman or trust her, but I'm his future wife. He should be able to trust me.

I want him to know that I'll always listen to his desires, give him what he needs, because I care about his happiness as much as he cares about protecting my happiness.

The coat slides off my shoulders, pooling at my feet. Cool air hits the bare skin of my shoulders. Goosebumps paint my skin, all the way down to my stomach. The smattering of pubic hair on my mound makes me self-conscious, but that evaporates when he licks his lips like he wants to eat me from the inside. He's honest, a little wild, but whenever I'm with him, all his attention is on me.

He makes me feel special and desired. At home, I pass by like a ghost, never seen or acknowledged by my parents or brothers. It's like I don't exist.

But when I'm alone with Mikhail, the whole world seems to be focused on me.

I'm left bare in his apartment doorway, my heart

hammering as Mikhail's eyes drag down my body in one slow, devastating sweep.

My nipples pebble into hard buds as cold air sweeps over my skin. The low temperature makes my pussy contract. But the coolness only makes the insides of my body radiate heat.

My breasts are heavy and hot at once as his eyes linger on my chest. His jaw tightens. I remember how good his mouth felt pressed against my needy tits. His tongue made electric sparks shoot through my pussy when he flicked it against my hard, needy peaks.

I arch my back, pushing out my chest at him. "Don't just look. Suck on it."

His breath comes harsher, heavier, but his voice is low, controlled, a dangerous purr. "You look so fucking delectable. I want to suck your pretty titties until you're crying in pleasure, but don't forget who is in charge here." His gaze snaps to mine, sharp and unyielding. "You think I'm powerless, just because your body gets me hard instantly?"

I swallow, heat searing through me at the way he says powerless, as if the word tastes like poison.

"Don't get it twisted, malyshka," he continues, crowding me back against the wall with the weight of his body. His chest presses into mine, hard muscle pinning me in place. "I still have the power. And now, I'm going to show you what that means."

My lips part to answer, but he takes my jaw in one large hand, tilting my head back until I can't look anywhere but at him. "First, I'm going to kiss you until your lips are swollen, until you can't even remember what it feels like not to have me on your mouth."

He doesn't wait. His lips crash into mine, his tongue sweeping deep, claiming, teasing, tasting. He kisses me until I'm dizzy, until I whimper against him, clutching at his shirt like I'll fall apart if I let go. But even then, even when he has pressed his tongue against every surface inside my mouth, sucked on my lip enough to make me feel lightheaded, he's not satisfied.

He bites my bottom lip. A sharp current of pain lances through my body, pooling in my pussy, inciting a new wave of moisture. My cunt tightens as if he touched me directly. My clit blooms with need, and the icy air heightens my arousal.

"Like that, malyshka? I'm going to bruise your lips. Every time you speak, you'll feel me and remember what we did. That's going to keep your pussy nice and wet all day tomorrow." He laughs, a pure, evil laugh that reverberates through my bones. "If you can't take being a dripping mess, you're welcome to come to my office and beg me to fuck you."

"You're a villain." I hiss, even as he nibbles on my lip again, sending a flurry of ecstasy into my grasping pussy. The emptiness in my cunt is getting too much to bear, but I know begging him will only make him play more games with me.

Mikhail peels back as the sting in my lips becomes a dull throb. My pussy clenches in time with that hot ache. He traces the shell of my ear, tilting his head with amusement. "Didn't you say you liked villains?"

Yes, I said that.

I scrunch my nose. He swoops in, holding my face like it's something precious as he licks the places where he bit me. Then he bites me again. My head jerks, but he holds it in place. He sucks hard, so hard I'm certain I'll feel that in my nervous system for days. I lose myself to his kiss. My mind blanks out as he alternates between giving me pain and pleasure, erasing every thought from my head. All I know is hunger. All I feel is need. All that pumps through me is anticipation, the need to know whether he'll soothe me, suck on me, or bite me next.

My thighs become slippery with leaking arousal. I've never gotten so wet from a kiss, and Mikhail is not stopping. I whimper into his mouth, locking my arms around him, pressing my tits to his chest, hoping to entice him.

His thick, hard cock, protruding through his pants, teases my soaked slit. I rub myself against him because I'll go mad if I don't get relief. The whispers of heat that flare in my groin in response to the friction between us drag me down to an abyss of pure rapture. I forget where I am. My muscles slacken. I let Mikhail push me against the wall and hold me, making sure I don't collapse because the one who has lost control of my body is me.

When he finally pulls back, his thumb strokes over my damp lower lip, his eyes dark and wicked. He grins, impressed by the damage he has caused. I should hate him for this, but being marked in such a primal, possessive way sets all my nerves on fire.

Mikhail makes me feel alive, needed, wanted. That's why I came here tonight. To reassure myself that he needs me. To experience this chemistry that defies everything, making us pawns in its conquest for explosion.

He's always the most sexually alluring when he's being darkly rough and dominant, teetering on the precipice of losing control. I like his wild, unhinged side, because that's a side of him I never got to see.

He pinches my chin between his fingers. When his calloused fingertip skims over my bruised lip, I jerk in pain. My lip feels raw. It throbs, but that throb only heightens the emotions inside me.

I never imagined it was possible to experience such unabashed, dangerous passion with a man. He expands my world, shaking up all my notions regarding sex and pleasure.

He kisses my cheek. "Good girl. You took that so well."

That single sentence, that single endearment, makes everything that he put me through worth it. I'll wear my bruise like a badge of honor tomorrow, knowing it made him happy. Mikhail Antonov is not a man who praises easily.

"Now that's done, I'm going to put you on your knees, right here against the wall, and watch you look up at me while I undo every button on my shirt. You'll wait, trembling, begging for me, until I decide you've earned it."

My muscles turn into liquid, and I slide down to my knees. The need to be submissive, to earn more of his praises, lashes through my stomach like a hunger pang. It's a cramp, a physical ache. His words, filthy yet spoken with deep passion and meaning, stir a longing in my groin. My core lights up as if someone lit a flame inside my body.

A shiver wracks through me. "Misha..."

"Shhh. Just watch, sweetheart." He undoes his buttons with cold precision. His eyes are dark yet smoldering with heat. The feral promises within those pupils have my pussy walls vibrating with desire. I need to know more of his domination, to feel the full force of his hunger. "Watch how hard my cock is for you."

He undoes his belt slowly. He acts like a man with power. His cock is so swollen it might rip a hole in his pants. Yet, he doesn't let his physical urges pull the strings. He takes his time, unzipping his pants, sliding them down his thick, muscled legs.

Saliva drips out of my mouth. It's an involuntary reaction to seeing his physique. He's stunning, corded with muscle everywhere, with legs that are so thick, I could hump them for days and be satisfied with just that.

But that thought evaporates when he pulls down his boxers, revealing his impressive, veined cock. His balls are huge, filled with semen that he's going to put inside me soon.

"You're such a filthy little fiancée, drooling for your husband's cock." He pumps his cock, then pushes the tip against my lips, collecting the saliva dripping out of my mouth.

He uses that as lubrication, rubbing it all over the crown. "Now get up, so I can stuff you full of my dick."

I come to my feet instantly. I'm eager to obey his requests because my pussy is going to combust until he stretches my walls with his thick cock and makes the incessant clenching go away.

He chuckles darkly, shifting my thigh up over his hip, grinding against me so I feel every inch of his arousal. "I was thinking of carrying you to my bed. I'll spread you out, tie those pretty wrists to the headboard, and keep you there until you're crying for release. But you're so desperate, maybe I should take you against the wall first."

His hand slips lower, gripping me hard enough to make me gasp. My slick dampens his skin, and his skin radiates heat into my folds. "You think you can control me with a smile, with a little tease? No, Zorina. I'll remind you who has the control here. Who decides when you fall apart."

My breath hitches, a desperate moan slipping out before I can bite it back.

His cock presses between my fat pussy lips. He drags it up and down, bathing his erect length with the moisture clinging to my slick folds. He brushes against my clit and entrance. Waves of pleasure ripple through me. I close my eyes, leaning into that feeling, into the pure bliss of having my slit stimulated by the tip of his cock.

Mikhail leans in, lips brushing the shell of my ear, his voice a whisper of sin. "The wicked part, little one, is I'll enjoy every second of teaching you that lesson."

My legs tremble, the world blurring around me until there's only him—his promises, his weight, his power pressing into me like gravity itself.

And God help me... I want every wicked thing he just promised.

His strong hands grip my thigh, lifting my leg and wrapping it around his waist. My back presses against the cool wall, the contrast of the cold surface and the heat of his body sending a shiver down my spine. I can feel his cock, hard and ready, pushing against my entrance. His eyes meet mine, a wicked grin playing on his lips.

"You wanted this, didn't you?" he murmurs, his voice a low growl that vibrates through me. "Wanted to feel my cock deep inside you."

I nod, my breath hitching as he presses the tip of his cock against my pussy, teasing me with slow, circular motions. My hands grip his shoulders, nails digging into his flesh as I try to pull him closer.

"Please, Misha," I beg, my voice barely a whisper. "I need you inside me."

He chuckles, a dark sound that sends a thrill through me. "Patience, malyshka. You're so eager, but you need to learn to take it slow. To savor every inch."

He thrusts into me, inch by inch, filling me so completely that I can feel him hitting every nerve ending. My body stretches to accommodate him, the sensation a mix of pleasure and pain that leaves me gasping. He's so deep, deeper than anyone has ever been, and the feeling of him hitting my cervix sends explosions of pleasure behind my eyes.

"See how good it feels when you can take me deep?" he grunts, his forehead pressing against mine. "I'm going to mark every inch of your pussy with my cock."

I cling to him, my legs shaking as he starts to move, his cock sliding in and out of me with slow, deep strokes. Each thrust hits that spot deep inside me, sending waves of rapture crashing through my body. I can feel every ridge, every vein of his cock as he stretches me, fills me, ruins me.

Heady sensations curl in the base of my stomach. My core

flares every time his cock's head touches my womb's entrance, making brutal promises.

The tension inside me balloons into a hard pressure that throbs in my gut, demanding to be set free.

"God, you feel so good," I moan, my nails raking down his back, leaving trails of red against his skin. "I've never felt anything like this."

He smiles, a feral grin that promises more to come. "That's because you've never had a real man fuck you, Zorina. Not until now."

His thrusts become harder, more insistent, each one pushing me higher, closer to the edge. I can feel my orgasm building, a pressure that threatens to consume me. My body trembles, my breath coming in short, sharp gasps.

"You're close, aren't you?" he whispers, his teeth grazing my earlobe. "I can feel your pussy tightening around me. You're going to come so hard, malyshka. And I'm going to enjoy every second of ruining you."

I cry out, my body arching against his as pleasure explodes behind my eyes. It's like nothing I've ever felt before—an out-of-this-world orgasm that leaves me speechless, breathless, disembodied. I float in another world, a world where only pleasure exists, where only he exists.

He doesn't stop, doesn't slow down. Instead, he picks up the pace, his cock driving into me with a force that has me seeing stars. His teeth sink into my earlobe, a sharp pain that only intensifies the pleasure.

"Fuck, your pussy just gripped me so hard. I can't stop myself anymore," he groans, his body tensing as he reaches his own climax. "I'm going to fill you with my cum, Zorina. Going to push it deep into your womb and knock you up."

His words send another wave of pleasure crashing through me, and I feel his cock pulsing inside me, releasing his seed deep into my body. He thrusts harder, deeper, driving his cum into me, making sure every last drop fills me completely.

I'm left speechless, breathless, my body trembling with the force of our connection. He's taken everything from me—my control, my reason, my ability to stay in my own body.

My organs are liquid. My nerves stopped feeling everything after he overloaded them with ecstasy. My blood pumps lazily, rushing to my core, feeding off the incredible sensations spiraling in my pussy.

Misha has stamped every part of my body with his dominance. And all I want is another round.

But when I look up at him, there's guilt on his face. He's staring at my lip. It must be starting to go purple or brown or something because the blood drains from his face.

He brings his finger to my lips, but withdraws it without making contact with my skin. "I'm sorry," he mutters. That's the second time the great, invincible Mikhail Antonov has apologized to me.

"What's wrong?" I ask, blinking back tears of intense pleasure. My body is reacting in all sorts of ways after reaching that incredible climax.

Mikhail pulls out. "Your face...your lips...I think it might scar."

There's a haunted look on his features. His expression bares his soul-deep anguish. He's already blaming himself. He's my fiancée but he's also my boss. If there are bruises on my face, it'll be visible during my performances.

His hands shake at his side. He closes his eyes. I see the self-recrimination flooding through his mind in the tight twist of his jaw. He grinds his teeth, taking one more step away.

My heart beats in panic. It took everything to get close to him. And now he's stepping back, putting distance between us again.

"It's okay," I tell him, grabbing his wrist. "I can hide it with makeup."

"I should have been careful. It's my fault. Fuck. This is why I shouldn't ever let passion consume me. I'm not...I feel like a monster. I don't know how to apologize to you, Zorina."

I hug him hard. I kiss his cheek. "Don't look at me like that. Like you regret what we did."

"Zorina...you can't go out looking like that. People will think I hit you." His arms lock around my waist. He nuzzles his face against my neck. "But that's not even the real problem."

"There's no problem!" I emphasize. "We had sex. It was rough. Intense. And I enjoyed it. I might have to wear five layers of makeup for a few weeks, but it's not the end of the world."

"No, you don't understand. This is bad. I got too...intense." Mikhail sighs. "I was afraid something like this would happen. Oh my God, I knew it was a bad idea to fuck you when I was feeling so much. This is even worse than last time."

The blood drains from my face. "Last time? Did something like this happen before?"

I mean, it has never happened when we had sex. But he must have had sex with other women before. I never asked, because honestly, I didn't want to know. Didn't want to imagine him with someone else.

I know Mikhail hides a lot from me. I barely know anything about his past. He was already thirty when we were engaged. His parents died when he was around eighteen. He must have endured a lot in life in his twenties, seen things I can't even imagine.

"Please tell me." I squeeze his hand. "What happened? Why are you so scared?"

Mikhail shakes off my hand. His shoulders stiffen.

For a minute, he doesn't say anything. I'm scared I'm going

to lose him again, lose the closeness we found. When he lifts his head, his expression shuttered, I have a feeling he's going to tell me to leave.

But then he surprises me by saying, "I guess you deserve to know. You're going to be my wife. But let's get dressed first. I want you sitting down when I tell you."

SEVENTEEN

Mikhail

I SIT on the edge of the bed, elbows braced on my knees, watching her slip into my shirt while I drag a hand down my face. My chest feels tight. Too tight.

Her lip is swollen, already turning a faint purple. A bruise, small but obvious. My doing. Again.

She pads over, barefoot, the hem of my shirt brushing her thighs. She looks so damn fragile in my clothes, but she's not fragile at all. Not where it counts. Her strength is in her eyes, steady and unflinching as she kneels in front of me.

"Misha," she whispers, resting her hands on my thighs, "tell me."

I shake my head, staring at the floor. "You won't like what you hear."

"I'll decide that."

Her voice is soft, but it cuts through me like a blade. I take a deep breath, forcing the words out.

"Before you, I had...someone. Not love. Just sex. She wanted rough, and I... I gave it to her. But I lost control." My hands curl into fists. "I strangled her. It was consensual. She wanted me to, but I went too hard. She lived. But I left marks. Dark ones, around her throat. She hated looking at herself afterward. Hated looking at me. Called me a beast who couldn't control his passion."

The words taste bitter, like bile. I've carried them for years, heavy as lead.

I can't forget about that incident. After that, I locked away my passion. I decided my life would be better without sex, because sex would always bring shame and guilt afterward. It would make me feel worthless, like a brute who didn't deserve to live.

So I suppressed that part of myself. I didn't touch any woman, not even my fiancée. I didn't want her to see this side of me. I was even ready to avoid sex even after we were married. But when I saw her with Victor, the guilt that had chained me all these years was shattered by the all-consuming passion and possessiveness I felt toward her.

She broke my chains, and now she'll pay the price for it.

"I don't know when to stop," I rasp. "That's why I didn't want to touch you. Why I thought it best to wait until marriage. Because once I start—" I break off, clenching my jaw. "I get carried away. And it's not fair to put that on you."

Her hands slide up my thighs, warm and steady. "So all this distance...all your coldness... it was because you were protecting me?"

I nod once, shame burning through me. "It's okay if you want to change your mind, Zorina. You don't have to marry a man who can't keep his hands gentle. I know you said you didn't want to be abused. I don't want you to do anything that you'll regret later."

For a moment, I can't look at her. But then her hands are on my face, cupping my jaw, tilting my head up. Her eyes glisten, full of stubborn fire.

"Misha," she whispers, "come here."

I resist, but only for a second. Then I cave, letting her pull me forward until my forehead rests against her chest. Her fingers slide into my hair, stroking softly, grounding me.

"It's okay," she says, kissing the crown of my head. "All women are different. I'm not afraid of a few scars. You've got way more than me, anyway."

A rough laugh breaks out of me, shaky, almost teary.

She kisses me again, firmer this time, her lips brushing mine. "I know you don't mean to hurt me. You only want to give me pleasure. I'll never think less of you for losing control, because it only proves how much you feel."

Emotion clogs my throat. I don't know what to say. I don't think I've ever been this close to crying in my adult life, but here I am, holding onto her like she's the only thing keeping me together.

"You look so fragile," I murmur, my voice rough. "But you're strong. Stronger than I'll ever be. I'm lucky I found you."

She smiles, brushing her thumb over my cheek. "And I'm lucky you let me in."

I swallow hard and pull away reluctantly. If I stay in her arms, I'll never get up again. And her lip is looking worse by the second.

I grab the first-aid kit from the drawer, my hands steadier now with a task to focus on.

"Sit still."

She obeys, perching on the edge of the bed. I disinfect her lip carefully with gauze and antiseptic, then apply a thin layer of antibiotic ointment, bacitracin, the kind my family doctor always insisted on for cuts and bruises.

She hisses at the sting. I blow lightly over her mouth, gentling her the way I wish I could always gentle her.

"There," I murmur, brushing her hair back from her face. "Better."

The tenderness surprises me. I like it. I like caring for her. It makes me feel...useful. Like I'm not just built for violence. Like I can be something else, something softer, for her.

When I look at her again, emotion rises sharp in my throat. I can't push it down this time.

I realize, in the silence stretching between us, that I'm in love with her.

With her fire. With her strength. With the way she accepts the darkest parts of me without flinching. She surprises me at every turn, and I want to spend the rest of my life discovering what else she'll reveal.

God help me. I think I finally found my reason to believe in something more than survival.

And that reason is Zorina Morozova.

I promised myself I'd never fall in love, never let a woman become my weakness. But here she is, my fiancée, breaking me with her soothing hands and accepting words, teaching me the meaning of tenderness.

And I can't even hate her for it.

She kisses me again, gentle, lingering, soft as forgiveness. Her lips brush over mine like she's reminding me I'm not the monster in my head. When she pulls back, she whispers, "I'm not going anywhere, Misha."

Something inside me loosens, a tension I've carried for years. I don't deserve the way she says it. With such certainty, such warmth. But I can't bring myself to push it away. My hand finds hers. I hold it, turning it over, running my thumb over her knuckles. I've never been a man who sought comfort in touch, but hers... hers feels like an anchor. Warm. Alive.

Every second, my love for her grows heavier, filling me until I don't know where to put it.

"Stay the night," I say, rougher than I intend. "Sleep next to me. If you're hurting, I'll call a doctor. I want to take care of you."

She smiles, stroking my jaw. "I'm fine. But yes... I'd like to sleep with you."

We settle onto the bed, side by side. She curls into me, her back fitting perfectly against my chest. I spoon her, my arm slung over her waist, keeping her close. The scent of her hair seeps into me, calming something primal.

We talk in the dark, the way only people do when the night makes them honest.

"Your album," I murmur. "How's it going? Have you written any songs yet?"

She sighs. "Slower than I expected."

"You'll get it," I say without hesitation. "You're a genius. You'll come up with something great."

A soft laugh escapes her. "You're the only one who believes that." She rubs her thumb over my knuckles, quieter now. "You're the only one who ever believed in me."

The words cut deep, both pride and ache tangled inside them. I squeeze her hand. "Don't feel so grateful you think you need to stay with me for that reason."

She twists just enough to look at me, her smile playful and defiant. "I'm not staying with you out of gratitude. I'm staying because the sex is good."

I huff out a laugh, tugging her closer, pressing my face into her hair. Her playfulness is light in my chest, addictive. I want her to always sound like this—teasing, happy, free. "You're impossible."

"Mhm," she hums. "And curious. Women like me and my mother...we're never treated as more than sexual objects meant to bear children. Never pleasured. Never cared for. If you had been the kind of man who only took from me without giving anything back... I'd already be gone."

Her voice lowers, almost mischievous. "But you're not like that. So I want to find out how many more orgasms you can give me."

Her words spark heat low in my gut, but it's her tone—half-tease, half-truth—that hits me hardest. She's reframing everything I hate about myself into something she wants, something that makes her stay.

I chuckle against her shoulder, my hand splaying protectively over her stomach. "So now I'm the sexual object. You only like me for the orgasms."

She laughs softly, and I feel it vibrate through both of us. I know what she's doing, steering me away from hating my own intensity, reminding me she craves it.

And damn her, it's working.

I hug her tighter, kissing her hair, silently vowing to keep that smile on her face.

WEEKS PASS, and life takes on a rhythm I didn't know I could have with someone.

Zorina throws herself into her music, spending long hours at the studio. I give her space, telling myself she needs her focus, that I shouldn't weigh her down with my hunger. I've learned to keep my hands off her before her concerts—no matter how much she tempts me—because I can still see that night burned into my memory, her purple lip, the guilt in my chest.

But something shifted after I confessed my fear. It's lighter between us now. I can talk to her without second-guessing every word, every move. She teases me in texts, sends me silly emojis when she knows I'm in a boring meeting. Every dinner, every conversation, every touch builds inside me, a pressure I can't contain.

I love her. I know it with a clarity that knocks me sideways.

But I'm not ready to tell her. Not yet. I want her to fall in love on her own, to know she isn't just tied to me by family or obligation. So I wait, swallowing down the words that burn my throat every time I see her smile.

Two months later, she invites me to the studio to hear her latest track. "The title track," she'd said, voice bubbling with excitement. "It's for a movie tie-in. You have to come."

I arrive with a box of cupcakes and her favorite matcha latte. The second she sees me, she squeals, and the sound hits me like a fist to the chest. She looks at me like I've brought her the world, when all I did was bring sugar and tea.

Her joy undoes me.

"Cupcakes and matcha?" she beams, bouncing on her toes. "You're spoiling me, Misha."

I can only stare, drinking her in. Every expression of hers feels like too much now. Too bright, too alive. It shakes me down to the marrow.

My gaze lingers on her mouth. She notices.

"You've been more distant since that day," she says softly, fingertips brushing over her lips. "You should forget about it. I already have. There's no scar."

Her eyes are steady, unwavering.

I nod slowly. "I'll try." My voice comes out rougher than I want. "Now play for me. I had a boring meeting, and I need something worth my time."

She laughs, settling her violin under her chin. And then she plays.

The music fills the room, sweeping me under like a tide.

Her bow moves with precision, but the sound is wild, emotional, alive. Every note carries her fire, her longing, her dreams. My chest aches listening to it. I could drown in this, in her.

When she lowers her bow, she looks at me expectantly.

"You're extraordinary," I say, and I mean it. "But..." I tilt my head, motioning. "Slow that middle passage down just a touch. Let it breathe. Make them feel it."

She nods, smiling. "You're right."

She's never once resisted my critiques. She takes them in, folds them into her music, makes it better.

"Are you free tomorrow?" I ask.

She hums, packing her violin away. "Just the studio. Perfecting tracks. Why? Do you want to take me on a date?"

Her smile is teasing, but I shake my head. "Actually, we're going to Moscow."

Her brows shoot up.

"For your bridal fitting," I add. "Leo got us an appointment with the same couturier who made our mother's gown. And Lena's."

Her lips part. Wonder flickers across her face, quickly followed by excitement. "Really?"

"We'll take a long weekend. Get away from everything for a bit."

"I can't wait," she breathes. "To try on wedding dresses."

My hand finds hers almost without thought. I bring it to my lips, kissing her knuckles. "I can't wait to call you my wife."

Her cheeks flush, and my chest tightens, because every damn expression she makes now—every blush, every laugh, every soft look—it hits me like a ton of bricks.

And I know, with a bone-deep certainty, that I'll never stop falling for her.

EIGHTEEN

Zorina

MY STOMACH TURNS the second the jet lifts off the runway. I excuse myself to the bathroom, slipping inside while Misha is engrossed in a call with one of his men. The nausea crests too fast—I fall to my knees and retch into the toilet, clutching the cool edges of the porcelain.

When it's over, I rinse my mouth, splash water on my face, and stare at my reflection. Pale, shaken. My lips bloodless.

It has to be the jet lag. Or something I ate. Nothing else.

When I return to my seat, I pretend to nap. I don't eat. I don't want him to notice, but his eyes flick over me now and then, sharp and knowing. He doesn't say a word.

By the time we land in Moscow, my stomach is still a knot. Mikhail takes my hand as we step off the jet, his palm steady, anchoring.

"Straight to the fitting," he says. "I can't wait to see you in your gown."

I manage a weak smile. "You can't look until the wedding day."

His brow furrows. "Then who's going to help you pick?"

"I called Lena," I reply, adjusting the strap of my bag on my shoulder. "She's meeting us there."

"Lena is pregnant," Mikhail says flatly.

I raise a brow, deadpan. "Her brain still works."

The corner of his mouth twitches. "Aleksei will kill us both if she goes into labor while she's picking your dress."

I laugh, though it makes my stomach twist. "That won't happen."

He doesn't look convinced. His hand brushes down my arm, lingeringly protective, before he leads me to the car.

When we arrive at the atelier, he stops at the curb. "I'll wait outside," he says firmly. "I won't look. Promise."

I nod and step out, smoothing my coat over my dress.

And then I see her.

Lena is standing on the sidewalk, radiant despite the cold. Her dark hair is swept up neatly, a soft wool coat wrapped around her curves, her belly prominent beneath it. In her arms is little Anechka, her daughter, and my future niece. She's two years old now, with a cute nose, expressive eyes, and cheeks flushed pink from the Moscow air.

The sight hits me straight in the chest.

"Let me take her," I say quickly, stepping forward. "You must be tired."

Lena's grateful smile warms me. She transfers Anechka into my arms, and I cradle her close, kissing her soft curls. My heart swells, my throat tightening.

"Ah, malyshka," I whisper in Russian, rocking her gently. "So beautiful. My little princess."

Anechka wriggles, reaching for my necklace. I grin. "If you watch me try on a few dresses, I'll buy you candy."

Lena laughs softly. "You've already discovered her weakness. You'll be a good mother someday."

Her words settle in me like a secret I don't want to name. Could everything I've been feeling—nausea, exhaustion, the odd ache in my chest—mean what I think it does?

It's too soon. It has to be too soon.

And yet, holding Anechka, I can't help imagining what it would be like to cradle a child of my own. A child with Mikhail's dark eyes, his stubborn mouth.

But if I am pregnant, everything changes. Marriage would come sooner. My career—my album, my tour—might end before it begins.

I press another kiss to Anechka's curls, hiding the war in my chest behind a smile.

Together, Lena and I walk into the atelier. The scent of expensive fabrics and flowers fills the air. A man in a tailored suit approaches, his presence commanding. The designer himself, here to oversee my fitting personally.

"Dobro pozhalovat', Miss Morozova," he says with a bow. "We'll make sure your gown is nothing less than perfect."

The atelier is like stepping into another world. White marble floors gleam under soft golden lights, and gowns float on mannequins like they belong to goddesses, not women. The designer guides me to a private room with a mirrored wall, velvet chairs for Lena and Anechka, and racks of silk and lace that whisper when the assistant brushes past them.

I step into the first gown. It has long sleeves of embroidered lace, the neckline modest and high, the skirt flowing in layers of satin that sweep the floor. It feels heavy, almost suffocating, like the weight of tradition wrapped around me.

When I step out, Anechka's eyes go wide. She claps her little hands and giggles, "Krasivaya!" Pretty.

My chest warms at her excitement. Lena smiles kindly but

tilts her head. "It is elegant. But too much like something your father would choose. You look beautiful, but where are you in this dress?"

She is right. I see myself in the mirror and all I can think of is my father's disapproving eyes, judging, controlling.

The second gown is simpler. A-line, white crepe, boat neckline. Safe. Respectable. Forgettable. Anechka yawns halfway through clapping, and Lena chuckles. "Even she thinks this one is boring."

I laugh softly, but my heart sinks a little.

The third is a ball gown with a fitted bodice and a full skirt of layered tulle. It reminds me of the princess dresses I used to dream of as a girl. Anechka squeals and kicks her legs, reaching toward me like she wants to bury her face in the skirt.

"She likes this one," I say with a small smile.

Lena strokes her belly, watching me closely. "It is sweet. But Zorina, you have a figure many women would envy. Why hide it under all this fabric? My body doesn't let me wear things like that right now, but yours was made for them."

I hesitate, my hands smoothing down the wide skirt. "My family... my father... he would never let me wear something strapless, or fitted, or anything that showed too much. I grew up with those rules."

Lena leans forward, her gaze firm but kind. "But you're not just his daughter anymore. On that day, you'll be Mrs. Antonova. Mikhail's wife. You can wear whatever you want. You'll only marry once, in a couture gown once. Choose for yourself. Pick the gown you want to wear, not the one everyone else expects of you."

Her words sink deep into me, loosening the fear that clings to my ribs. I've never had a sister, but in this moment Lena feels like one, lifting me up, urging me to step into who I could be, not who I was told to be.

"Then let me try something else," I say, emboldened. I step back into the fitting room and point to a gown on the rack that glitters faintly under the light. "That one."

The assistant brings it over. I slip into it, heart pounding.

The gown hugs me like a second skin. Sheer panels with intricate embroidery trace my torso, while the sweetheart neckline leaves my shoulders bare. The skirt falls sleek and smooth, pooling around my feet in a shimmer of silk. It is daring. Bold. Everything my father would hate.

When I step out, Anechka's mouth drops open. Then she erupts into giggles, clapping wildly. "Teta Zorina krasivaya!" Aunt Zorina pretty.

Heat floods my cheeks as I stare at my reflection. For the first time, I don't see the shadow of my father's rules. I see me.

Lena's eyes soften. "Now that is a bride who knows herself. It looks incredible on you. But..." she leans back, a smile tugging her lips, "try more. Try everything you want."

The next gown takes my breath away for a different reason. It is simpler than the last, ivory silk with a fitted bodice and a flowing skirt, the neckline delicate with scalloped lace. Something about it reminds me of the dress I wore to my very first violin performance. My mother had bought hurriedly, complaining about how she never signed up to be a stage mom. It was simple and unadorned, but to me it was magical. Wearing this feels like stepping back into that moment, except now I am stronger, older, ready for the stage of my life.

When I look in the mirror, I see more than a bride. I see the girl I was, and the woman I am becoming.

This gown reflects my past and present. The girl who grew up with dreams of playing the violin and the woman marrying the man who gave her dreams wings.

I want my wedding gown to be more than a pretty dress. I

want it to be meaningful and sacred. When I look back at it, I want to remember the woman I was when I got married.

Lena's hand presses over her heart. "This one. You shine in this one."

Anechka toddles over, wrapping her little arms around my legs. I bend, hugging her close, my heart swelling as she buries her face against the gown and giggles.

"Yes," I whisper, kissing the top of her head. "This is the one."

The designer smiles at me, pleased. "Understood, ma'am. We will get started on your measurements. I must say, you made an excellent choice."

The decision is made, and the assistants bustle around me, pinning the gown in places, murmuring in French and Russian as they note every adjustment. Another seamstress crouches to mark the hem, her pins clicking softly against the fabric.

"Just a few measurements so it will fit you perfectly," the designer assures me with a smile.

I nod, but my chest tightens.

What if I grow? What if I really am pregnant, and my body changes before the wedding? Will I even fit into this gown? I picture my father's face, livid, spitting his fury that I'd ruined everything.

Mikhail would be different, I'm sure. He would want the child. He would be proud. But then what about our wedding? Would it be delayed again? Would he resent me for it?

The thought makes me lightheaded.

When the seamstress tugs the tape snug around my waist, my stomach flips. I swallow hard, pressing a hand to my lips.

"Zorina?" Lena's voice cuts through the haze, steady and gentle. "You look pale. What's wrong?"

"Nothing," I lie quickly, forcing a smile.

But the moment I step off the fitting platform, the nausea

hits sharp and sudden. I turn away, retching into a handkerchief the assistant thrusts at me. My cheeks burn with humiliation.

Lena is at my side in an instant, her hand rubbing soothing circles over my back. Her eyes narrow in that way only a mother's can. "Are you pregnant?"

My stomach clenches harder. Panic flares in my chest. "I... I don't know."

Her brows lift. "You and Mikhail have been together...?"

I nod quickly, biting my lip. Heat scorches my cheeks. "But please... don't say anything. I don't want to tell him. Not until I know for sure. He worries too much."

Lena's expression softens, and she pulls me into a warm embrace, stroking my hair. "It's all right. Don't cry. I'll get you a test. Tonight. After I put Anechka to sleep, I'll come to your room. You guys are staying with Aleksei and me at the townhouse for the night. We'll find out together."

Tears sting my eyes. Relief pours through me at her quiet, unwavering support. "Thank you," I whisper against her shoulder. "You're so nice to me. I can't wait."

When we leave the atelier, Lena's driver and bodyguard are waiting to see her and Anechka safely into their car. She kisses my cheek before she goes, squeezing my hand in reassurance.

I watch the car pull away before heading toward the curb where Mikhail's black sedan waits.

The window lowers, and he leans out, arching a brow. "I thought you were going to spend the entire day inside."

I slide into the seat beside him, smoothing my dress. "I picked a gown I like."

His eyes soften, and he nods once. "Good. I'm glad."

Before I can say more, he pulls me into his arms and kisses me, his lips rough and hungry, making the world tilt on its axis.

And for a moment, even with the storm of uncertainty in

my chest, I let myself melt into him, savoring the taste of his kiss and the safety of his arms.

NINETEEN

Mikhail

THE ANTONOV DINING room is intimate, not ostentatious. Heavy drapes soften the glow from the chandelier, and the long oak table gleams from years of Galina's polish. The scent of her cooking drifts through the air. The table contains an extravagant spread of borscht with fresh dill, baked pirozhki, and pelmeni swimming in butter. These are the meals of my childhood, and for a moment, sitting here again, I feel almost at peace.

Zorina sits across from me, quiet at first, her fingers toying with the edge of her napkin. I've noticed her distance since we landed. She'll sleep in the guest room tonight, as expected. Appearances matter. My brother and his wife don't know we're having sex. As is expected of arranged marriage brides, I want them to think Zorina came to me pure during our wedding night.

Still, when we're together, she keeps slipping away. Eating

little. Hiding her thoughts. Latching onto Lena like a baby chick chasing warmth. She seems to be pulling away from me, almost like she can't face me and I don't understand why. I don't think I've said or done anything to upset her. Does she just need space?

At dinner, though, Galina's food works its magic. I catch Zorina dipping bread into her soup, taking seconds of pelmeni, even laughing when Aleksei teases her about her appetite. Relief loosens my shoulders.

"Zorina is making progress," Aleksei says, smirking over his glass of kvas. "She'll finally eat something. Unlike my brother, who looks at food like it offends him."

I grunt, pushing pelmeni onto my plate. "I eat."

Lena leans into Aleksei, her eyes sparkling. "Not like normal people. He acts as if emotions—even hunger—are beneath him."

Zorina chuckles, covering her mouth. "I think he feels more than he admits."

I roll my eyes, but when I glance at her, she's smiling at me softly, like she knows something I don't.

Anechka wiggles on her chair, reaching for me. Without thinking, I lift her onto my lap. She grabs my tie, yanking it toward her mouth.

"Devchonka," I mutter, tugging it back. "Your papa is saying terrible things about Uncle Mikhail. What do you think about that?"

She blinks at me, solemn for a moment, then turns to her father. "Papa, stop being mean to Uncle Mikhail."

The table erupts in laughter. Even Galina, shuffling in with more bread, hides her grin in her apron. Aleksei groans, muttering something about betrayal, and Lena pats his arm in mock sympathy.

I find myself laughing, too, rumbling low in my chest as

Anechka pats my cheek like she's just defended my honor. When I glance across the table, Zorina is watching me. Her eyes are full. Tender, shining with an emotion I can't name.

Does she want this? A child in her arms? My child? Does she dream of me holding our child one day, lavishing her with the love I give my niece?

The thought digs into me, both dangerous and warm.

I shift Anechka into Zorina's lap. She hugs the little girl tightly, pressing kisses to her curls. Her face lights up as she and Lena start chatting about baby toys and sweets. I sit back, listening quietly, trying not to let the sudden rush in my chest overwhelm me.

Lena turns, smiling. "Mikhail, we're planning a special night. Zorina and I will stay up late, eat junk food, and watch movies. A girls' sleepover. You and Aleksei aren't invited."

Aleksei groans again. "You're heavily pregnant. You should be sleeping, not staying up to gossip."

Lena pouts, resting a hand on her belly. "I never meet women my age to have fun with. Let me enjoy this."

He sighs, defeated, kissing her temple.

I clear my throat. "Zorina has a flight in the morning. She needs rest, too."

Zorina shakes her head, smiling. "I've caught plenty of flights without sleep during my European concerts. One night won't kill me."

I study her carefully. She wants companionship. I can see it in the way she leans into Lena, the way her face softens when Anechka hugs her. And I appreciate Lena for giving her something I can't—sisterhood, friendship, female warmth.

Still, when Zorina absently rubs her stomach, my mind stutters.

I can't help wondering.

Is it just nerves? Or could it be something else?

THE WALLS ARE thick in Aleksei's penthouse, yet I can still hear the bursts of laughter from the room next door. Zorina and Lena are supposed to be watching movies, but I hear no music, no television. Just muffled voices, too fast and nervous, then silence.

The silence unsettles me more than the laughter.

I lie in bed, staring at the ceiling, but my mind won't rest. My body craves her. She has become a part of my nights, of my life. I never thought I would be the man who could not sleep without a woman beside him, yet here I am, restless without her warmth tucked against me. She is already irreplaceable.

Another minute passes. Still nothing. The silence feels wrong.

I swing my legs off the bed and walk into the hallway. The floor is quiet, hushed. Aleksei must be downstairs putting Anechka to bed. The soft tick of the grandfather clock is the only sound.

I knock on the girls' door, sharp enough to be heard.

A shuffle inside, then the door opens. Lena stands there, petite with her dark hair loose, one hand at her belly. Her face is tight, worried.

"What is wrong?" I ask, looking down at her. My height lets me peer over her shoulder into the room, but I do not see Zorina. My chest clenches. "Where is she?"

Lena opens her mouth, hesitating, but before she can speak, the bathroom door bursts open.

Zorina stumbles out, eyes wide, voice high with shock. "Oh my God, I'm pregnant."

The words slam into me.

For a heartbeat, I cannot breathe. Then it floods in—

elation, disbelief, awe. I push the door wider, my voice breaking. "What?"

She pales instantly, lips trembling. Lena steps back, murmuring, "I was just about to shoo you away."

I glare at her, fury sparking. "You knew she was pregnant?"

Before Lena can answer, Zorina rushes forward, grabbing my arm. "No, she didn't know. She only suspected. She bought the tests for me, but we weren't sure until now."

Her voice shakes. She looks terrified, not of the test, but of me.

I wrap my arms around her, holding her tightly. "Why did you not tell me?"

She presses her face against my chest, her voice muffled. "I was scared."

"Scared of me?" I whisper, stroking her back.

Her silence cuts me, but I force myself to soften, rubbing her stomach gently, then up her spine. I bend and kiss her hair, then her lips. "I would never blame you. I would never hate you for this. Thank you for growing our baby inside you."

Her shoulders shake. Tears spill down her cheeks.

Alarm shoots through me. I cup her face, wiping at the wetness. "Why are you crying? Do you hate this? Do you hate being pregnant?"

Lena touches my arm, murmuring, "I will leave you two alone." She slips out quietly, closing the door.

I sit on the edge of the bed, pulling Zorina onto my lap. She sobs, clutching my shirt. I pat her back, whispering steady words. "It is okay. You have not done anything wrong. Nothing."

Between sniffles, she shakes her head. "I want this baby. I do. I was just so overwhelmed. It all hit me at once."

Relief punches through me. I kiss her, then lower myself to

kiss her stomach reverently. "Do not worry about anything. I will take care of you. Both of you."

She sniffs again, looking at me with watery eyes. "We'll have to move up the wedding. Early next year. My father will not like me showing in a gown."

"As much as I would love to see you pregnant in white, you are right," I admit, brushing my thumb over her cheek. "We will marry sooner. Before it shows."

Her lips wobble. "I thought I had more time. Now I cannot tour. I'll be too big by then."

"We'll reschedule the tour," I say firmly. "The album can release before the wedding. After you have the child, you can go on tour. You have been making great progress."

Her gaze flickers, guilt weighing her down. "Won't I have to quit my career after the wedding? I told you I would. My father will expect me to be more traditional. A Bratva wife cannot also tour the world. I cannot take care of the house and be rehearsing at the same time."

I tilt her chin up, pressing a kiss to her mouth. "Listen to me. There are no real responsibilities of being a Bratva wife. The staff runs the house. We can hire nannies. You can even take the baby on tour, or only perform locally for a while."

Hope blooms in her eyes, dilating her pupils, but it's quickly overshadowed by darkness. Zorina pulls her shoulders in, dropping her gaze to the floor. "What about events? You're a businessman. I'll have to always be on your arm as your wife. It would be frowned upon if I'm always missing and you have to make excuses for me."

"Firstly, I don't attend many social events. Only business meetings, which you cannot be present at anyway." I place my hand on her head. She looks at me through vulnerable, wide eyes. She's so adorable. I want to put her on my lap and kiss her senseless. But before that, I need to assuage all her fears. Zorina is terrified right now. Of what she has to lose by having our baby. I have to reassure her that she will lose nothing. "As for events, I can always tell people my wife is busy being brilliant. You are famous. They will understand. You have never accompanied me to any events even when you were my fiancée."

Her voice is a whisper. "It might make you look bad."

I shake my head. "I do not care how I look. I care that you never regret this child, or think it took something from you. You are signed to my label. I am your boss. And your boss says you should tour after you have recovered, and after we have spent time with our child."

"Yes, boss." She hiccups. "I'm glad you're my boss."

"Just your boss?"

She reaches up, wrapping her arms around me, pressing a chaste kiss to my lips. A thrum of electricity rolls through my skull. I love any physical contact with her, even something as cute as a kiss.

"My husband. My child's father. I'm glad it's you."

She clings tighter, her tears soaking my shirt. "I am glad it is you. I was so afraid you would expect me to sacrifice everything. That you would not support me."

I hold her closer, voice rough. "You are already sacrificing enough. Your health, your body, carrying my child. I cannot ask for more."

She lets out a shaky laugh, blinking through her tears. Her eyes shine up at me. "I would marry you right now if I could. You are the best man I could ever wish for. I never thought an arranged marriage could give me freedom, understanding. This is not what Bratva marriages are supposed to be like."

The words rip out of me before I can stop them. "I love you."

She freezes, staring up at me.

I kiss her again, fierce and unguarded. "I love you, Zorina.

You will have everything you need. You will never worry again. Just focus on yourself, and our baby."

She sniffles, nodding against me.

"Tomorrow we go to the doctor," I say, already planning, already determined. "We will make sure you are fine."

Her hand covers mine on her stomach, trembling but steadying under my touch. "Yes."

And for the first time in years, I feel it. Hope.

The room is bathed in a soft glow from the bedside lamp, casting a warm light over Zorina's face. She looks up at me with those wide, innocent eyes, and I can't help but feel a swell of emotion in my chest. This woman, this incredible creature, is carrying my child. Our child. The thought sends a wave of possessiveness and pride through me. I want to shout it from the rooftops, declare to the world that she is mine, that she carries my legacy within her.

"I can't believe this is happening," I murmur, my hand gently stroking her stomach. "You, me, a baby. It's more than I ever hoped for."

She smiles softly, her hand covering mine. "It feels surreal. I keep thinking I'm still dreaming."

I lean down, kissing her stomach reverently. "You're going to look so beautiful, swollen with our child, leaking milk from your breasts, nourishing them at your tits. I can't wait to see it."

She laughs nervously, her fingers tracing patterns on the back of my hand. "I'm going to look fat and ugly."

I place a finger on her lips, silencing her. "You'll look radiant. The way a wife should look when she's been bred and given a baby to carry."

Her eyes widen, but she doesn't protest. Instead, she leans into my touch, her breath hitching as I trail my fingers down her body, hooking them into the waistband of her pajama bottoms. I tug them down, exposing her to me, and she lifts her hips to help.

"I want to feel the cunt I bred," I growl, my voice low and rough. "I want to taste it, to reward you for being such a perfect breeding bitch."

She gasps, her cheeks flushing with a mix of embarrassment and arousal. I push her legs apart, spreading her wide for me, and lower my head. The scent of her arousal hits me, sweet and intoxicating, and I groan as I lean in, my tongue licking a long, slow stripe up her slit.

"God, you taste so good," I murmur, my fingers digging into her thighs. "Like home. Like the mother of my children."

She moans, her hips bucking against my mouth as I tease her clit with my tongue. I lick and suck, drawing out a gasp from deep within her. Her hands fist the sheets, her body trembling as I bring her closer to the edge.

Just as she's about to come, I pull back, a wicked smile playing on my lips. "Not yet, malyshka. I want to feel you come on my cock."

I stand up, my eyes never leaving hers as I undress. Her gaze roams over my body, hunger burning in her eyes. When I'm naked, I climb onto the bed, my cock hard and ready. I grab her wrists, pinning them above her head, and grind against her, feeling her slick heat against my length.

"You're so wet for me," I growl, my voice ragged with need. "So ready to take my cock."

I slap her thigh lightly, a sting that makes her gasp. "Can't wait for you to gain weight on these thighs. You're going to look properly pregnant. Everyone will know you belong to me. That your womb has been claimed by me."

She whimpers, her hips arching up to meet mine. I thrust into her, hard and deep, filling her completely. She cries out, her body tensing around me, and I groan at the sheer perfection of it.

"Fuck, you feel so good," I grunt, my hips moving in a brutal rhythm. "So tight, so perfect."

I grip her wrists tighter, using them as leverage as I drive into her. Each thrust hits her cervix, and I can feel it, the fluttering of her womb against my cock. It's a reminder, a primal claim that I put my baby inside her, that I claimed her.

"You're mine, Zorina," I growl, my voice harsh with possession. "Every inch of you. Every part of you. You belong to me."

She moans, her body arching against mine, her breasts pressing against my chest. I release one of her wrists to cup her breast, squeezing the tender flesh, feeling the hardened peak of her nipple against my palm.

"These are going to be so full," I murmur, my voice thick with desire. "Full of milk for our baby. I can't wait to see them, to taste them."

She shivers, her body clenching around me, and I know she's close. I thrust harder, deeper, my cock slamming into her cervix with each powerful stroke.

"Come for me, Zorina," I command, my voice rough with need. "Come on my cock. Show me how much you love being bred by me."

She screams, her body convulsing around me as her orgasm rips through her. I feel her pulsing, her inner walls clamping down on my cock, and it sends me over the edge. I come hard, my cock pulsing deep inside her, filling her with my seed.

We breathe in unison, staing like that for minutes, just feeling each other. Her velvet pussy walls ripple around me. I don't want to leave her cunt. I want to stay inside her all night, stay connected to her and the life we created together.

I kiss her tenderly, my hands stroking her body, soothing her as she comes down from her high. I roll us onto our sides, my cock still buried inside her, and pull her close, my arms wrapping around her.

"I love you," I whisper, my voice soft and gentle. "More than anything. More than life itself."

She sighs, her body melting into mine, her head resting on my chest. "I love you too, Mikhail. So much."

I stroke her hair, my fingers trailing down her back, tracing the curve of her spine. I can feel the steady rhythm of her breath, the beat of her heart against mine. This is perfection. This is everything.

"Sleep, malyshka," I murmur, my voice a soft rumble. "Sleep knowing that you are loved, that you are safe, that you are mine."

She nuzzles into me, her body soft and pliant, and I know that she is drifting off, her dreams filled with the promise of our future together. As I hold her, my cock still buried deep inside her, I know that this is where I belong. This is my home, my sanctuary, my everything. And I will protect it, cherish it, and love it until the end of time.

TWENTY

Zorina

THE DOCTOR'S words still echo in my head. Healthy. Strong heartbeat. Our baby is doing well.

It feels surreal every time I touch my stomach. Tonight, I smooth a hand over the satin fabric of my dress, light gold that clings just enough to remind me of the small secret I'm carrying. Misha has not let me lift a finger since he found out. He brings me food, keeps an arm around me when I get tired, watches me with the same fierce focus he once used to intimidate me. Only now it feels protective. Loving.

My parents do not know yet. Mornings at my house have turned into a careful dance, me avoiding breakfast, claiming I have no appetite so they will not notice my changing body or the nausea that still lingers. But mornings are easier now. The worst of the sickness has passed.

Mikhail is already planning. He told me he will speak to my father soon and move up the wedding. It should comfort me, but it is still strange to think that everything I have ever wanted is actually happening.

He told my father tonight that there would be a New Year's Eve event at his house. Yet when I walk through the front doors, the place is silent. No guests, no murmurs of conversation, no clinking glasses. Only the soft hum of music from the hidden speakers and the faint scent of pine from the wreaths hanging in the hallway.

I turn to him, confused. "Where is everyone? Where's the party?"

"There is a party," he says with a hint of a smile, taking my hand. "But it is only for us."

He leads me through the house, past the quiet rooms, out toward the back. When he opens the glass doors, the air catches in my throat.

The garden and pool shimmer in the night. Strings of fairy lights glow along the hedges, wrapped around trees, draped like a canopy overhead. The reflection glitters in the still water of the pool, and candles flicker on tables set out by the garden. The whole place looks like it was plucked out of a dream.

He kisses my hand and pulls out a chair for me, every inch the gentleman. "You cannot drink anymore, so I will not either."

I sit, touched by the gesture. "I don't mind if you have wine."

He shakes his head, his eyes softening in a way that still startles me. "I am already drunk. On your face. You glow, Zorina. I do not need alcohol."

My cheeks heat, and before I can respond, the chef appears. He carries in two plates, setting them down in front of us with quiet precision. The first course is delicate, almost too pretty to eat. A tower of smoked salmon layered with avocado mousse, dotted with caviar and edible flowers. Tiny golden blinis on the side, along with a drizzle of citrus sauce. Crystal glasses are filled with water, sparkling in the fairy lights.

I lift my fork, tasting the first bite. It melts on my tongue. "This is incredible."

"Only the best," Misha says, watching me instead of his food.

I savor another bite, letting the flavors distract me. For a while, it is just us, the clink of cutlery, and the hush of the garden.

How far we have come. I glance at him, at the way he looks across the table, relaxed in his chair yet utterly present. He was once so cold, distant, a man I thought I could never reach. Now I cannot believe he is the same man. He is going to be a father. My husband.

"I am happy too," I whisper, setting down my fork. "To be a mother. I have always wanted a family of my own. My family..." My chest tightens. "It was never warm. But I want ours to be different. A home full of laughter and chaos."

He chuckles, the sound deep and warm. "That suits you. You should be surrounded by children who need you, who love you. You are too nurturing to be alone."

Heat floods my cheeks, especially when I feel his foot under the table, rubbing against my ankle. I fumble with my napkin, flustered. "They are not swollen yet. I am not that far along."

His smile curves. "I am practicing for later."

I melt at his words, my heart turning to liquid. He can be rough, ruthless when he wants to be, but when he is tender, it undoes me completely.

"I never thought I could have this," I blurt before I can stop myself. My voice wavers with honesty. "I never thought I could have this kind of openness, this kind of pleasure, with my husband."

He watches me, his eyes dark and steady, and I feel it again—that sense that I have stumbled into something rare, something I never thought belonged to me.

"I'm sorry if I made you feel that way in the past." My heartbeat explodes with the shock of his apology. "I was trying to avoid you because I didn't want to hurt you, didn't want you to see what I become when I'm in the throes of passion. Also, you were too young. I couldn't take away your innocence before you had lived your life."

His fingers dig into my heels, softly kneading my aching foot. I sink into the blissful feeling of his hands on mine, of him giving me this small, tender measure of affection. "I understand why you did it. It was the right thing to do. I'm not blaming you. I *was* too young."

"But now you're a woman. A beautiful, ripe, glowing, pregnant woman carrying my child. And I want you more than ever."

Heat snakes up to my cheeks, spreading across my face. "I want you, too. I think pregnancy has made me hornier."

"I'm glad to hear that." He licks his lips, nodding decisively. "Because I have a lot planned for tonight. After we watch the fireworks, I'm going to make fireworks explode inside that pregnant cunt of yours. I want to feel the pussy I bred, feel our baby inside you."

His words hit me squarely between my legs, making my pussy clench in anticipation. That, coupled with his gentle ankle massage has me wet and squirming before the next course arrives.

The second course arrives in elegant silence, served by the chef himself. Perfectly seared scallops rest on a bed of risotto, dotted with truffle shavings and garnished with microgreens. The scent is intoxicating, rich yet delicate.

I take a bite, closing my eyes at the buttery texture, and

when I open them, Mikhail is watching me with that small curve of his lips that feels rarer than any jewel.

"Why are you looking at me like that?" I ask, heat rushing to my cheeks.

"Because I can," he says simply. "Because you are mine to look at."

My heart gives a dangerous lurch.

I busy myself with the food, trying to ground my thoughts. Yet the question slips out anyway. "Do you ever... dream about the future? What do you want your future to look like?"

He leans back in his chair, eyes never leaving me. "You."

I freeze, fork in midair. "Me?"

"Yes." His tone is matter-of-fact, but his gaze is burning. "I dream of having you every night. Of building a family with you. A beautiful family."

Something trembles deep inside me, fragile and yearning. "I want that too," I whisper.

The corners of his mouth soften. "And I dream of attending your concerts with our children. Sitting in the front row, showing them how amazing their mama is. For giving life to them, and for playing such soulful music."

A laugh bursts out of me, but my throat tightens. "I might not still be playing by then."

"You will." His voice is quiet, steady. "I know you. Music is in your blood. Even if you stop for a while, you will always return to it. You are a creative soul, Zorina. You cannot shut that off."

He is right. I know he is right. My eyes sting as I smile across the table. "You know me better than I know myself."

He tilts his glass of water toward me, as if in a toast. "For six years, I never showed you love. But I was always watching. Always observing."

Six years of him, silent in the shadows of my life, studying me. And now here we are, closer than I ever thought possible.

I grin, trying to lighten the heavy emotion in my chest. "Then one day, I'll bring our kids to your office. Show them their father, the sexy businessman who provides for our lifestyle."

He chuckles, shaking his head. "Do not. They might discover I am not just a businessman."

The word bratva hangs unspoken, but his smile eases the weight of it. I giggle, reaching across to tap his hand.

The third course arrives, tender beef medallions with a red wine reduction, accompanied by roasted root vegetables and potatoes carved into delicate spirals. We eat slowly, talking about the future in whispers between bites.

"I want us to take vacations," he says suddenly. "Even when we have children. I do not want you to feel neglected."

My lips part. "You mean... just us?"

"Yes. You will not come second to them. You are my wife. I will make sure you always feel like it."

The sincerity in his voice punches straight into my chest. My heart feels too full, overflowing. He is giving me everything I once thought was impossible—love, respect, partnership.

I realize, with startling clarity, that I am in love with him.

By the time dessert arrives, a chocolate soufflé that melts into molten perfection with the first spoonful, I am dizzy from more than the sugar. I am dizzy from him. From us.

When the plates are cleared, he rises and takes my hand. His palm is warm, steady, grounding. He leads me upstairs, through the quiet house, into his room.

The balcony doors are open, letting in the crisp night air. He steps behind me, his arms wrapping around my waist, his chest pressing into my back. The city skyline stretches before us, lights glittering like stars. And then the first firework explodes across the sky, painting it in red and gold.

We watch as the night bursts into color. Greens, blues, purples, all crackling and echoing over the city.

His lips brush my ear, his voice low and rough. "Happy New Year, wife."

My heart flips.

He presses a hand to my stomach, his other arm banding around me. "This year, we become parents. We become husband and wife. Everything changes."

I turn my head, meeting his gaze over my shoulder. "It will be the best year of our lives."

"Da," he murmurs, kissing me deeply as another firework bursts overhead. "The best year."

We stand together, bathed in the glow of the fireworks, holding on as if the world belongs to us.

THE NEXT FEW days pass in a haze of unexpected bliss.

Mikhail comes to the studio every afternoon, carrying little surprises. One day it is a box of macarons, the next a container of borscht Galina made. He hovers in the control booth while I play, or sits silently on the couch with a file open on his phone. Sometimes he looks at me over the top of the screen, his dark eyes unreadable, and I feel a flutter low in my stomach that has nothing to do with the baby.

When my nausea returns, he is there instantly, holding my hair back, his palm rubbing gentle circles on my spine until the wave passes. His suits always smell faintly of his cologne, clean and woodsy, and I find myself pressing into his chest afterward, letting him absorb the worst of my weakness.

This afternoon, I am curled in a chair with my violin

resting against my knee when he crouches in front of me, eye-level. His tie hangs loose, his sleeves rolled up, his hair slightly disheveled from running his hands through it. The sight of him like this—untamed, softer—makes my heart squeeze.

"How are you feeling?" His voice is gentle, but his eyes search me, probing for cracks.

"I'm fine," I say quickly, brushing a stray curl behind my ear. "I'm about to start recording, and things are going well."

But my voice wobbles, betraying me. He tilts his head, not buying it.

"You look nervous." His hand finds mine, his thumb tracing the inside of my wrist.

I swallow. "It's just... at home, it's hard. I feel like I'm always walking on eggshells. Afraid to slip up and have my parents find out before I'm ready."

He leans closer, pressing a kiss to my temple. "You don't have to live in a home like that anymore. Not when you're carrying my baby." His hand slides to my belly, resting there reverently. "If you're unhappy, if you're stressed, it will affect the baby too. I won't allow that."

Guilt prickles at me. "I'm sorry."

His eyes sharpen, and he shakes his head. "Never apologize for this. It isn't your fault. It's mine. I should have seen it sooner. I should have corrected it."

I meet his gaze, my heart hammering. "Corrected what?"

"That you're still there." He strokes my cheek, his calloused thumb dragging softly over my skin. "Move in with me, Zorina."

The words are firm, decisive, the way he says everything. My breath catches. "Misha... my father would never allow that."

"Our wedding is in three months," he counters smoothly. "I'll tell him you need to learn the skills to be my wife. That means knowing how to manage my household. It is a reasonable request."

I shake my head, half-laughing. "Manage your household? You have staff for everything."

His lips twitch, the closest thing to a smile. "He doesn't need to know that." He leans in, his forehead pressing against mine. "I'll visit your home this evening. I'll talk to him."

My heart stutters, fear and hope colliding inside me. "You would do that?"

"I would do anything to protect you and our child." His fingers lace through mine, tightening. "I cannot watch you suffer in silence."

I want to tell him I love him. The words burn on my tongue, heavier each day. He already confessed his feelings, steady and sure as he always is. But I, flighty and uncertain, still hesitate.

Not because I doubt. No, I am certain now. The way he looks at me, the way he touches me, the way he has transformed the cold distance into warmth and safety—I am falling in love with him more every second.

I just want to tell him when I can make it unforgettable.

"Misha..." I whisper, my hand rising to trace the strong line of his jaw. His stubble scratches lightly under my fingertips, and the heat in his eyes makes my knees weak. "You really mean it, don't you?"

He cups my face, kissing me slow, deliberate. "Every word."

I melt into him, my fingers twisting into his shirt, clinging because I cannot get close enough.

This man—my fiancé, my protector, the father of my child—has become my everything.

TWENTY-ONE

Mikhail

SPEAKING to Vadim always takes years off my life. The man is inflexible, rooted in a world that is already dead. Every word is a battle. Tonight was no different. But in the end, I got what I needed. He agreed, grudgingly, that Zorina could stay with me. His conditions were predictable. A chaperone. Separate rooms. The charade of propriety.

I agreed, of course. I intend to follow none of it.

I'm glad Zorina is going to leave that horrible home tomorrow. I'll get to sleep beside her. But my days of dealing with Vadim aren't over. He'll be my father-in-law. If anything, we'll be seeing more of each other once I get married. I hate to think how that will affect Zorina. When it comes to light that she's pregnant and it's clear she got pregnant before marriage, I hope he doesn't judge her for it.

I'm half considering moving to Moscow for the duration of

Zorina's pregnancy so we don't have to see her father when I park outside my mansion.

When I step into my house, loosening my tie, I expect silence. Instead, I see my eldest brother standing by the bar, a glass of water in his hand.

Leo Antonov does not need introduction. He carries the air of command like it is stitched into his skin. Broad-shouldered, perfectly groomed, with eyes that see too much and a calm that hides a ruthless mind. Where Aleksei looks like brute force and Dmitry wears the arrogance of youth, Leo has always embodied control. Tonight, his jacket is draped neatly on a chair, his shirt sleeves rolled up, his posture unyielding even in relaxation.

I stop in the doorway. "What the hell are you doing here?"

He arches a brow, sipping. "Vadim called me."

I grind my teeth. "Of course he did."

Leo sets his glass down. "He says you're trying to move Zorina in with you. And that you moved up the wedding date."

"My wedding is my problem," I mutter, striding past him to pour myself a drink. The whiskey burns down my throat, but it does little to settle me.

"It's my problem, too," Leo says. "I'm the one who arranged this peace treaty between the Morzovs and Antonovs. My neck will be on the line if anything goes wrong."

"You don't have to worry. She's going to marry me. She agreed to it," I reply flatly.

Leo's voice cuts through the silence. "Why the sudden change, Misha? A few months ago, you couldn't stand to be in the same room with her. Now you're moving mountains. Why?"

I say nothing, staring at the amber liquid swirling in my glass.

His tone sharpens. "Are you in love with her?"

I shrug, the smallest concession I can give.

Leo's eyes narrow. "There's more. Tell me, so I can manage the situation before it spins out of control."

Despite his domineering nature, he is not just the pakhan. He is my brother. And for that, I trust him.

"She's pregnant." The words fall heavy, and for the first time, I feel lighter for saying them aloud. "I don't want her in Vadim's house, being belittled and stressed. It's not good for her. Or the baby."

Leo exhales slowly, steady but thoughtful. "Does Vadim know?"

"No," I snap, meeting his gaze. "And he will not find out. Not until after the wedding. I will not have Zorina criticized."

His lips twitch. "You're very protective of her."

"She's carrying my child," I growl. "Why wouldn't I be?"

He studies me, long and hard. Then he shakes his head. "I didn't expect this. I'd have preferred you two waited."

"Everything doesn't work according to your plans," I bite out, sharper than I intended.

For once, Leo actually looks surprised. "So you really..." He smirks faintly, almost amused. "I didn't think you'd touch her before the wedding. I'm glad you did. She brought your passion back. You seem... different. More human."

"Fuck off," I mutter, though I feel the truth of his words.

Leo chuckles, unbothered. "Fine. I'll tell Vadim that I agree it's best for her to stay here. He'll trust my word on it."

I set my glass down with a clink. "Thank you."

He pats my back, solid and warm. "We're brothers. I'm grateful for everything you've done. You kept the businesses alive when our parents died. You made them thrive. I don't forget that."

"Now that I have a family of my own, I'll be making even more money," I say dryly.

He laughs, genuine this time. "I like the sound of that. And I can't wait to call Zorina my sister-in-law."

We lock eyes, and for once, there is no tension between us. No power struggle. Just mutual understanding.

Leo has always been more authoritative with Nikolai, Aleksei, and Dmitry. But with me, it has always been different. We're equals, because I carried as much weight as he did when we were younger, and because I never bowed to him, even when he took the title of pakhan.

"I'm glad I trusted you to arrange my marriage," I say quietly. "You picked the best bride possible."

He leans back, smug. "I am always right."

I snort. "This is exactly why Nikolai thinks you're an insufferable tyrant."

Leo only smirks, his silence an admission of guilt.

For the first time in a long while, I feel the faintest thread of peace. My woman is safe, my child will be born into security, and my brother—our pakhan—stands with me.

THE DAY she moves in feels like a turning point.

When I open the front door and see her standing there with her suitcase, a soft sigh escaping her lips, I know I made the right choice. Relief is etched into her features, her shoulders lighter than I have ever seen them. For years I watched her smile in public, watched her posture shift into poise and performance, but this—this is real. The unguarded joy of freedom.

It does something to me. Warms the cold parts I thought were permanent.

I take the suitcase from her and set it aside. My hand goes immediately to her waist, guiding her inside. "Welcome home."

Her eyes glisten, and I cannot help myself—I lean down,

kissing her. She melts against me, small and warm, her fingers curling into my lapel.

"I like the sound of that," she whispers when I pull back.

"You'd better," I say, pressing another kiss to her forehead. "You're not leaving."

She laughs, and the sound echoes through my house, filling the empty spaces with something alive.

I keep my hand on her waist as I lead her through the rooms, unwilling to let go now that I can touch her freely. Every curve, every shift of her hips under my palm, makes my chest tighten. I never imagined I would crave something as simple as closeness.

"This is the living room," I say, gesturing to the wide expanse with leather couches and tall windows. "Where I'll watch you fall asleep on my lap after a long day. And where I'll carry you upstairs if you're too tired to move."

Her cheeks flush. "That sounds... convenient."

I grin. "For me, yes."

We move to the kitchen. I slide behind her, kissing the side of her neck as I speak against her skin. "This is where we'll eat as a family. Where I'll kiss your belly while you're cooking or feeding our children."

She shivers, her hand gripping mine. "Misha..."

"You like the idea?" I murmur, brushing my lips over her shoulder.

Her nod is small, but her body tells me everything.

I take her upstairs, pausing at the double doors of the master suite. "This is the bedroom we'll sleep in." My hand tightens on her waist. "This will be your favorite room, because this is where I'll fuck you every night."

She gasps, her face turning crimson, but the way her lips part makes me chuckle.

"Mikhail!"

"What? I'm being honest," I say, bending to kiss her hard before she can protest.

When I finally let her breathe, her eyes are glassy. "You're impossible."

"Da," I agree, pressing another kiss to her temple. "And you're mine."

I show her the office, the gym, even the library. Every room comes with a promise. A kiss on her lips, her throat, her hand. A murmur of what I plan to do to her here, with her, for her.

By the time we end the tour, she is flushed and laughing, her eyes sparkling in a way that makes my chest ache.

She is home. With me.

And I will never let her go.

TWENTY-TWO

Zorina

THREE MONTHS LATER...

I CAN'T BELIEVE I'm getting married today.

I stand before the tall mirror, hands resting lightly over my stomach. Thank goodness I'm now showing yet, but I feel the weight of the life inside me nevertheless. The gown glimmers like moonlight, every stitch hand-sewn to perfection. The bodice hugs my figure in just the right places, the neckline elegant without being immodest, and the skirt flows in waves of silk and lace, trailing behind me like a dream come to life.

This is the gown I chose months ago, the one I knew was mine the moment I slipped it on. Seeing myself in it today, my wedding day, feels surreal. Not only because I am marrying Mikhail, but because I am carrying his child. Our child.

Since I moved in with him, life has been heaven. I never

knew pregnancy could feel so cherished. He notices every detail—when I need water, when I crave strawberries, when my back aches, when my moods shift. He makes me feel adored, protected, celebrated.

"Zorina, that gown is too much. You should have chosen something more modest, something less... loud," my mother's voice cuts across my thoughts.

The familiar sting pricks at my chest, but before I can reply, Lena steps forward. Her tone is calm but cutting, steel wrapped in silk. "She looks perfect. She is marrying today, and she does not need criticism. Give us time alone."

My mother's lips pinch, but she leaves with a huff, muttering under her breath. Relief floods me.

I glance at Lena, unable to stop the tears that spring to my eyes. "Thank you."

She smiles softly, radiant even in her bridesmaid's dress of pale rose silk. Her hair is twisted elegantly off her face, but her eyes carry warmth and love. "You don't need to thank me. This is your day, Zorina. Nothing should taint it."

Before I can answer, Clara steps forward, her hand on mine. She looks luminous, her dark hair tumbling in waves over her shoulder, her figure just beginning to round with pregnancy. I know her secret because I was there, the night in Las Vegas when she and Nikolai found out. She is shy, but her eyes shine with happiness.

I pull them both into a hug, tears slipping freely now. "I love you both so much. I can't wait to be a real aunt to Anechka and Konstantin. And one day, to your baby too, Clara."

Lena laughs softly, her voice full of pride. "You'll be the best aunt. And the best wife. And you're always welcome in Moscow, Zorina. Always."

My throat closes up. I cling to her. "You don't know how much that means to me. To have real family. To have sisters. I can't wait for a girls' night with you, just us. No men, no stress."

Clara grins, cheeks flushed. "Can I join too?"

"Of course you can," Lena and I say in unison, and the three of us laugh through our tears.

My heart feels full, fuller than it has ever been. I came into this family as an outsider, but now... now I am theirs. And they are mine.

Clara squeezes my hand. "I listened to your latest album. It's beautiful, Zorina. I've been playing it while I study, and it makes everything easier. It's... grounding."

Joy bursts inside me. "Thank you. That's all I've ever wanted—for my music to mean something to someone."

Before I can say more, my father appears at the doorway, stern as ever in his black suit. "It's time."

His tone is clipped, his face unreadable, but for once, I don't shrink under it. My heart is too strong, buoyed by the sisters beside me, by the man waiting for me at the altar.

I look at Lena, glowing in her rose silk, at Clara, luminous in her pale lavender, both women standing as my bridesmaids because I have no friends of my own here. Yet, I feel supported. Loved.

This is my family.

And in a few minutes, I will walk toward the man of my dreams, the father of my child, the love of my life.

The doors open. The soft notes of a string quartet spill into the hall, mingling with the whispers of guests as all heads turn toward me.

My arm is linked with my father's, but I barely feel the weight of him. All I see is the man at the end of the aisle.

Mikhail.

He stands tall in a perfectly tailored black suit, the fabric molded to the breadth of his shoulders and the strength of his frame. His tie is sharp, his shoes gleam, but his eyes—they undo me. Dark, molten, locked entirely on me. For once, they are not cold or unreadable. They glisten, almost teary, as though holding back an ocean.

The sight makes my breath hitch.

Every step forward feels surreal, like I am floating. The lace of my gown trails across the polished floor, my veil shimmering under the golden chandeliers. Yet nothing could outshine the way he looks at me, as if the entire world narrowed to this single moment.

When I reach him, my father releases my arm, and Mikhail takes my hands. His palms are warm, steady. He leans slightly closer, his voice pitched for me alone.

"You look beautiful," he whispers, rough with emotion. "I cannot wait to love you for the rest of my life."

My heart twists, tears burning behind my lashes. "And I can't wait to love you back. Every single day."

The officiant's voice drones on in the background, but it feels far away. All I hear are his whispers, all I feel are his hands clasping mine.

As the vows are spoken, we echo them softly, eyes never breaking. His thumb strokes over my knuckles, anchoring me.

When it is time to exchange rings, his fingers tremble slightly as he slides the band onto my hand. I do the same for him, smiling through tears.

"You're mine now," he murmurs, low enough only I can hear.

"I've always been yours," I whisper back.

And when the officiant declares us husband and wife, Mikhail does not wait. He pulls me into him and kisses me with a hunger that silences the hall. It is not just passion—it is promise, devotion, and the sealing of everything we have endured to reach this day.

My veil brushes against his cheek, his lips firm yet reverent. Applause erupts around us, but I barely register it. All I know is the taste of him, the press of his hands at my waist, the feel of my future in his arms.

As I break away, breathless, I see it clearly.

I am safe. I am cherished.

I am loved.

And our future, whatever it holds, will be nothing short of extraordinary.

I'm crying by the time wedding is over, but I don't have the luxury of gathering my emotions. Because the very next moment, I'm being pushed into the wedding reception hall.

The reception hall glows with golden light, chandeliers dripping crystals above long tables dressed in white linen. The Antonov crest gleams in subtle embroidery on the napkins, and everywhere I turn, I see familiar faces smiling. But more than the guests, it is Mikhail's brothers who fill the night with warmth.

Leo raises his glass first, his presence as commanding as ever. "To my brother and his bride. May your marriage be as strong as the empire we built, and as enduring as our family."

Everyone echoes the toast, crystal clinking, and my chest swells with pride.

Aleksei follows, his grin softer than I have ever seen. He glances at Lena seated nearby, her eyes sparkling with pride, before looking at me. "Mikhail, you have always carried the weight of this family on your shoulders. Tonight, you've found someone who will carry it with you. Zorina, welcome to us. You are not just a wife. You are a sister, a daughter, a part of us now."

I blink fast, tears threatening.

Then Dmitry, playful as always, leans forward with his glass. "And here I thought Misha would never smile again.

Zorina, whatever you've done, keep doing it. He's less terrifying now."

Laughter ripples through the hall. Even Mikhail chuckles, though his hand squeezes my thigh under the table.

I laugh too, cheeks warm. They're not mocking me—they're welcoming me. And for the first time, I know my past is truly behind me. The lonely girl with no allies in her own home is gone. Here, I am celebrated. Cherished.

As the music swells and people return to their meals, Mikhail leans close, his breath teasing my ear. His voice is low, meant only for me. "Your dress is sinful. It shows every inch of you. I can't wait to taste it all once we're alone."

My pulse leaps. I shift in my seat, pressing my knees together, and his quiet chuckle makes heat coil low in my belly.

I feel his desire snaking around me like an invisible rope, tightening around my curves, making me feel his pulsing need for my body.

By the end of the night, my cheeks ache from smiling, my heart from holding so much happiness. The guests drift away, the music fades, and finally we are alone.

When we return to his house, my husband (I can't believe I get to call him that) lifts me in his arms without a word. My gown pools like silk waterfalls over his forearms as he carries me up the stairs. I loop my arms around his neck, breathless at the way he looks at me—like I am his prize, his treasure, his bride.

He lays me gently on the bed, kissing me deeply before his lips trail lower. He spreads the skirts of my gown, pressing reverent kisses to the swell of my stomach. "I'll worship you tonight," he murmurs against my skin. "You, and the life you carry."

My chest aches with emotion. Yet something else burns

hotter. "Misha," I whisper, curling my fingers in his hair. "I want you to be rough. I miss that part of you."

He shakes his head, lifting his gaze to mine. His eyes are fierce, protective. "You're pregnant. I won't risk it."

"That's why I need it," I breathe, arching into his touch. "I need all of you."

Mikhail's mouth stills against my skin. I can feel the tension in him, the push and pull of desire warring with control. His hands grip my hips, strong and unyielding, yet they tremble ever so slightly as though I have asked him for the impossible.

"Zorina," he rasps, lifting himself over me, his face shadowed with conflict. "You do not understand. If I lose control..."

I cradle his cheek, forcing him to look at me. "I do understand. I know what you're afraid of. But you would never hurt me. Not on purpose." My lips curve in a soft, daring smile. "And I need all of you tonight. Don't hold back, not from me. I'm your wife now. I carry all your burdens, too. I want every part of you, especially the dark and forbidden parts."

His jaw flexes, his gaze darkening with something that is both hunger and torment. He leans down, kissing me with a force that steals my breath. The kind of kiss that tastes of surrender, of love, of fear that he cannot protect me from himself.

When he pulls back, his forehead rests against mine, his voice gravel low. "You're going to break me."

"Maybe I'm meant to," I whisper. "Maybe that's what love is."

The growl that escapes him is raw, guttural. He tears the gown down from my shoulders, the satin slipping away like water. His hands roam over me, claiming, reverent yet hungry, as if he cannot decide whether to worship or devour.

His kisses descend from my lips to my throat, biting, sucking, leaving heated trails that make me whimper. I clutch his shirt, tugging, begging. "Please, Misha. I want to feel you. All of you."

He shudders, finally giving in. "Then you will."

He pushes my thighs apart, his fingers teasing me until I am squirming, moaning into his mouth. But even as his hunger builds, his other hand stays anchored at my belly, protective, grounding. "Tell me if it's too much. Swear you will."

"I swear." My words break into a gasp as he presses inside me, stretching me with that familiar, overwhelming fullness.

He groans, his mouth against my ear. "You feel better than heaven. Better than sin. I can't stop once I start, malyshka."

"Don't stop," I whisper fiercely, nails digging into his back. "Don't you dare stop."

He grabs my breasts, squeezing firmly but not harshly, cupping them in his large palms. His thumb brushes over my nipples, eliciting a gasp from deep within me. They are sore and ache with sensitivity—a common symptom of pregnancy. But his touch is gentle, reverent, as if he understands the delicate nature of my body's changes.

"You are so beautiful like this," he murmurs, his eyes fixed on my breasts as he massages them, his fingers circling the tender peaks of my nipples. "I can't wait to see these swollen and leaking with milk for our baby."

His words send a shiver down my spine, a primal response to his appreciation of my changing body. I arch into his touch, a moan escaping my lips as he continues to knead my breasts softly.

"They look so full, so ripe," he growls, lowering his mouth to capture one nipple between his lips. He sucks gently, his tongue swirling around the stiff peak, drawing out a gasp from deep within me. Then he bites down lightly, sending a jolt of pleasure mixed with pain through my body.

I cry out, my fingers tangling in his hair, pulling him closer.

He doesn't stop, moving to the other breast, lavishing it with the same attention. Suckling, then biting, then soothing the tender flesh with his tongue. The sensation is overwhelming, my body trembling with need.

"You're mine, Zorina," he whispers against my skin, his breath hot and heavy. "Every inch of you, every curve, every mark of our child growing inside you—it's all mine."

He trails his hands down my sides, gripping my hips as he flips me onto my stomach. His strong hands lift my hips, positioning me on my knees, my ass in the air. I can feel his gaze burning into my most intimate place, and it sends a wave of heat through me.

"I want to see this beautiful ass bounce as I fuck you," he growls, his hand coming down hard on my cheek, the sting sending a jolt of pleasure straight to my core. "I want to see your tits jiggle as I thrust into you from behind."

He lines himself up behind me, his cock pressing at my entrance. With a forceful thrust, he enters me, filling me completely. I cry out, my body convulsing around him as he begins to move, his hips pounding into me, each thrust hitting a spot deep inside that sends waves of pleasure crashing through my body.

"You feel so good," he groans, his hands gripping my hips tightly, his fingers digging into my flesh. "So fucking tight and perfect."

His thrusts become harder, more insistent, his cock plowing into me with a force that has me seeing stars. I can feel every ridge, every vein of him as he stretches me, fills me, ruins me.

His control frays, every thrust harder, deeper, sending sparks of ecstasy racing through me. Yet even in his roughness, he keeps one hand braced against me, steady and protective, as though reminding us both that I am carrying his future.

The room fills with the sound of our breathing, our bodies

colliding, my soft cries against his growls of pleasure. And somewhere in the chaos, I realize—he isn't just giving me passion. He is giving me trust.

He is giving me all of himself. His balls slap against my ass. The wet sound makes my belly clench every time. The tension trapped in my core tightens, as heat floods my system. The friction between his cock and my bare pussy walls is maddening. Sparks kiss my deepest parts every time he brushes his dick against my inner walls.

And I know, as my pussy sizzles with bliss, that I will never want anything less. I want all the wild passion and raw, intense sex that he will give me.

"Please, Misha," I beg, my voice breathy and desperate. My pussy can barely fit his huge dick. He has me stretched to my maximum capacity. Yet, with every stroke, he demands more. More submission. Access to deeper parts of my channel. And I give it to him. "I can't take much more."

He leans down, his lips brushing against my ear. "You can take it, malyshka. You can take all of me."

He wraps his hand around my throat, applying a light pressure that has me gasping. The sensation is dizzying, the danger of his hand around my throat coupled with the intensity of his thrusts tightening the tension in my belly. I feel wild and free, surrendering completely to his wildness, to his untamed passion.

"I want to feel your heartbeat against my hand as I fuck you," he murmurs, his voice rough with desire. "I want to feel how much I affect you."

He tightens his grip, just enough to send a surge of adrenaline coursing through my veins. My heart pounds against his palm, my breath coming in short, sharp gasps. The pressure, combined with the intensity of his thrusts, sends me spiraling toward the edge.

"Tell me you want this," he demands, his voice harsh and commanding. "Tell me you want me to fuck you like this."

"Yes," I gasp, my body trembling with need. "Yes, I want this. I want you to dominate me, to treat me like your possession, to show me what it means to be your wife."

His hand tightens around my throat, just enough to make me dizzy with pleasure. His thrusts become frenzied, each one hitting a spot deep inside that sends waves of ecstasy coursing through my body. I can feel my orgasm building, a pressure that threatens to consume me.

He leans down, his teeth sinking into my shoulder, a sharp pain that only intensifies the pleasure. I cry out, my body convulsing around him as the first waves of my orgasm crash over me.

"That's it, malyshka," he growls, his voice rough and possessive. "Come all over my cock. Show me how much you love it."

My body obeys, convulsing around his cock as pleasure explodes behind my eyes. I scream his name, my inner walls clamping down on him, my juices flooding around him. The sensation sends him over the edge, his cock pulsing deep inside me, filling me with his hot, thick seed.

He collapses on top of me, his body slick with sweat, his breath ragged. As he pulls out, he flips me onto my back, his eyes locking onto mine.

"I want to see your face as I kiss you," he murmurs, lowering his lips to mine, his kiss both tender and possessive.

He trails his lips down to my breasts, kissing the sore, aching flesh gently, lavishing them with soft kisses and soothing licks of his tongue. His hands squeeze my breasts, his fingers massaging the swollen flesh, his touch both gentle and firm.

"You're so beautiful like this," he whispers, his voice filled with awe and admiration. "I can't wait to see you fully pregnant, your tits leaking milk for our baby."

His words send a deep, primal satisfaction through me, a sense of belonging, of being cherished and desired. He makes me feel like the most beautiful, desirable woman in the world, and I bask in the warmth of his words and touch.

He moves back up to my lips, kissing me deeply, his tongue dancing with mine in a slow, sensual exchange. He wraps his arms around me, pulling me close, our chests pressed together as if we were one. The feeling of his hard muscles against my soft curves is heavenly, and I melt into his embrace.

"I love you," he whispers against my lips, his voice filled with raw emotion. "You're my wife, Zorina. Forever."

I smile against his lips, my heart swelling with love and devotion. "I love you too, Misha. You're my husband, the only man I'll give myself to without question. Forever."

He laughs, and the sound, so foreign, so infectious, is proof of how far we have come. He used to never let his guard down like this. But now I get to cherish his smiles, his grunts, his moans, and every other beautiful sound he makes. Just for me. All for me.

As we drift off to sleep, his cock lodged deep within my cunt, I know that this is the life I was meant to live. This is the connection, the love, the passion I have dreamed of, and Mikhail Antonov made my dreams come true.

EPILOGUE

Mikhail

Three years later...

PARIS GLITTERS outside the opera house, all golden light and hushed grandeur, but I barely notice the gilded ceilings and velvet seats. My world is much smaller, much softer, contained in the small weight perched on my lap.

My son squirms against me, his dark curls soft under my palm. He looks like me more than his mother, but I can see that he's going to be an artist already because he likes to play the piano at home. Leo likes to joke that he might fulfill Uncle Leo's dream of becoming a figure skater someday.

I press a kiss to his forehead. "Shhh, malysh. Mama is about to come on stage."

The lights dim. The velvet curtain stirs, then rises.

And there she is.

Zorina steps into the glow, her violin gleaming under the spotlights. The audience hushes, a reverent silence falling over the hall. She wears a midnight blue gown that clings to her curves, her hair swept back to bare the elegant line of her neck.

My breath catches. Even after all these years, after countless nights falling asleep with her curled against me, I am still spellbound.

"Ma-ma!" my son cries, reaching pudgy hands toward her.

"Shhh," I murmur, rocking him gently. He presses his cheek to my chest, still staring at her with wide, adoring eyes.

Then she plays.

The first note soars through the air, rich and haunting, and my chest tightens. I watch her bow dance across the strings, her body swaying with the music. She has given me so much—our child, our home, her laughter in the quiet mornings—and yet she still gives to the world, pouring herself into every note.

She carried our son, birthed him, and still took him on tour when he was small. She balanced the weight of being a mother and an artist, and somehow, she shines brighter than ever. She released an album just last month, already a success. Yet she always comes back to me, to us, to Las Vegas where we built our family.

I have killed, fought, and bled, but it was she who gave my life meaning.

After the final note fades and the ovation roars, I slip backstage, my son clutching my neck. We find her in the dressing room, glowing with post-performance fire.

"Mama!" he squeals again, lunging for her.

She gathers him into her arms, rocking him even though he is heavier now, his little legs dangling. He grabs greedily at her breasts, and she laughs, adjusting her bodice with practiced ease.

"Zorina," I murmur, drinking her in. She looks stunning—slim from the years after pregnancy, but soft again, curvy in a way that makes me think of the meals I insist she eat, the way

I've kept her well-fed and cared for when she's not constantly on tour. Her skin glows, her smile radiant, and I swear she's more beautiful now than on our wedding day.

She kisses our son's temple, then lifts her eyes to me. "How did you like it?"

He babbles nonsense, too young for sentences, but I step forward, cupping her jaw. "It was perfect. You were perfect. Every note was fire. You had them in the palm of your hand from the moment you touched the bow."

Her eyes soften, lips curving. "You're starting to sound like my biggest fan."

I press my mouth to hers, murmuring against her lips. "I am your biggest fan."

She kisses me back, our son giggling between us, wedged in the space of our embrace.

Then she leans close, whispering in my ear, her breath tickling. "I have something to tell you."

My brow furrows. "What is it?"

She takes my hand, guiding it down to her belly. Her smile trembles with joy. "You're about to be a daddy for the second time. I'm pregnant again."

For a moment, the world halts. Then elation floods me, fierce and bright.

I set our son carefully on the sofa, his toy clutched in his hands, and turn back to her. My body moves before thought—I press her against the wall, kissing her fiercely, passionately, tasting her laughter and her tears all at once.

"Spasibo, moya lyubov," I murmur between kisses. "Thank you for giving life to another miracle."

She cups my face, eyes shining. "You've always supported me, Misha. I want to grow our family, too. Give our son a sibling, so they can have each other." She coughs. "And we can have more time alone. Let them keep each other company. I want to be in my husband's arms more often."

I chuckle, resting my forehead against hers. "A very strategic woman. But you should know—" I kiss her again, slow and deep "—I will always spend time with you. Children or not. You will never come second."

Her eyes glisten, her arms sliding around my neck as our son babbles happily from the sofa.

In this quiet Parisian room, with my wife glowing in my arms and my son giggling nearby, I know without doubt.

This is everything.

Once, I thought love was a weakness I could never afford. Now I know it is the strongest weapon I will ever wield.

ALSO BY KRYSTAL CLARK

Loved this book? Read Book #1 in the series, Alekseia and Lena's story, a full-length dark mafia romance with breeding, pregnancy, college romance, and more: Pregnant for the Bratva Dom

Want to know what's next? Subscribe to my newsletter to be informed of new book releases and read exclusive excerpts. I release at least one book a month. You can be the first to know about sales, free ebooks, and special offers.

If you like longer novels with instalove, breeding, pregnancy, and lactation, start reading this steamy series with the first book: Knocked Up by My Ex's Dad.

Love highly erotic short stories with milking/lactation kink? Check out Stalker Daddy's Milk.

Want to read more books this this, filled with taboo romance, forbidden love, and intense sex? Start with the first book in this series, Hucow for the Priest.

I have written more than 80 books with plenty of age gap, daddy kink, breeding, lactation, dark romance, mafia romance, hucow, and BDSM stories. Check out some of my other works!

Dark, sensual, spicy romances with an intense, consuming love story: Dominant Daddy's Captive Bride.

If you're eager for short cowboy romance novellas with breeding, and other kinks, start my cowboy romance series with: Baby-making

Like omegaverse erotica? Check out: Knot My Fated Mate

Alien's Omega Captive (MM)

Bully's Rejected Omega (MM)

Buy my box set collections, which contain 15 of my other books focused on breeding, daddy kink, and lactation.

Milky with Big Bellies

Taboo Daddy Short Stories Collection

Taboo Pregnant and Milked

And my other short stories:

Pregnant for My Alien Ex

Degraded by My Best Friend's Dad

If steamy monster romances with breeding kink, lactation, and pregnancy float your boat, try:

Maid for the Gargoyle Lord.

My Best Friend's Monster Dad

Kraken King's Bride

Arranged Marriage with a Werewolf

A Nanny for the Lich

Demon's Secret Baby

Milked by the Dragon

ABOUT THE AUTHOR

Krystal Clark is the author of over 90 erotica, contemporary romance, and monster romance books. She writes hot and steamy stories with happy endings. She writes a variety of kinks, but her books often feature protective alpha males, lactation, pregnancy, and breeding kink. Get hooked to her addictive, high-heat romances today!

Printed in Dunstable, United Kingdom

68659131R10129